THE VI
APPREN

JOURNEY TO THE OTHER SIDE

THIRD EDITION

BOOK 3 IN THE VIKING SERIES

BY KEVIN MCLEOD

COPYRIGHT 2014 KEVIN MCLEOD

Kevin McLeod

#1 Bestselling Author of The Award-Winning Children's Series, *The Viking's Apprentice*

The Vikings Apprentice

The Vikings Apprentice II: The Master's Revenge

The Viking's Apprentice III: Journey to the Other Side

The Viking's Apprentice IV: The Sword of Vercelli

The Viking's Apprentice and The Master's Revenge are now also in audio book format. Please visit below to see how you can listen to these books for FREE on Audible:

www.kevinmcleodauthor.com/audible

For Rachael and Elena.

Prologue

'Issa, Issa! Come quick,' the children shouted, their voices full of excitement.

'What is it, children?' she replied as they dragged her by the hand, trying to get her to follow.

'They've come Issa. You must see!' the children cried.

Issa had never seen them like this. Their excitement was contagious, and she found herself being led through the forest.

'Where are we going children? You know never to leave the forest,' she said, becoming worried that the children had left the forest without telling anyone.

'We have to show you, it's on the water!' they called in response, never slowing down as they moved forwards.

The forest ended at the slope of a hill which ran down to a small stone beach. When Issa arrived, she found more children standing at the edge of the forest looking out to the sea. When they saw her, they ran to her. They were full of excitement and all taking at once. Finally, she was able to calm them down, and one of the older children spoke for the group.

'Look out to the water Issa. Is that them? Is that the ones you talk about in your stories?' The child asked the questions then pointed out to the sea.

Issa stared out to sea and took an involuntary step backwards. She regained her composure and looked again, this time moving closer. One of the children handed her a spy glass. She looked through it and brought the ship into focus. Issa gasped; a single tear rolled down her cheek.

'Is it them Issa? Is it them?' the oldest child asked.

'I believe it is, and they're coming this way,' she replied. She turned and looked at the children before continuing.

'We must be ready. If they've come to this world, then something has happened. They might need our help. Hurry children; we have to be ready.'

Issa began to half run back through the forest then turned to the oldest child.

'Yolundi, can you please stay here? Watch the ship and let us know when they make land.'

'Of course, Issa.'

With that, Issa ran off back through the forest to tell the other adults. The Viking had arrived, and she had much to prepare.

Chapter 1

As soon as they were through the portal, everything changed. Peter looked back as the portal closed and left their world behind. The strange purple sky with its dark red sun cast a strange glow over everything. It was hard, at first, for their eyes to adjust and the Vikings stopped rowing while they took in their new surroundings.

They looked for the Master's boat and saw it disappearing into the distance. A dense fog began to close in around it, and the boat was soon lost from sight.

'Where did they go? Did you see the way that fog came in?' Peter asked his Granddad.

'Remember Peter; this is not our world anymore. There's so much we don't know about this place,' Granddad replied.

'He knows, though,' George said, pointing at the troll who was tied up on board the ship.

'That's right. He can lead us straight to them,' Peter said looking at his Granddad.

'Why would he? How could we believe anything he told us? We'll need another way to find the Master now.'

Granddad watched the troll as he spoke and noticed a glance towards the shore in front of them. Granddad followed the gaze and moved to the front of the ship. He looked at the shore then back to the troll. A smile crossed Granddad's face.

'What is it?' Elder Sanderson asked.

'The troll was looking up at that forest,' Granddad replied, pointing towards the shore. He turned to the others and continued.

'Do you see something unusual?' he asked.

'Apart from the purple sky, weird sun and the fact that we're in another world?' George replied looking towards the forest.

'Yes George, apart from all those things. Look at the forest. When we were talking, and I mentioned finding another way to get to the Master he looked up at that forest.'

'So, what does that mean? He could've been looking there already.' Peter said.

'I don't think so, Peter. Look at the beach and the hill running up to the forest. What do you see?'

'Nothing it's all burned and dead.' Peter said before turning and smiling at his Granddad.

'The forest isn't burned or dead. It looks normal.' He continued.

'Exactly, so the question is why?' Granddad moved towards the troll and knelt down next to him.

'What's in that forest that makes it different?'

'I don't know what you're talking about.' The troll replied. Pus smacked off his lips as he spoke.

'You looked up there earlier when we were talking. There's something up there.'

'The only thing for you here, Viking, is death.' The troll sneered, then looked Granddad directly in the eyes.

'Don't you see? This is what she wanted all along. She wanted you in this world away from your house of tricks, and away from your guardians. If you try and save those children, you will die. Your only hope is to turn and go back through the portal.'

'We're not leaving without Charlotte and James.' Peter said, moving towards the troll. Porr put his hand on Peter's shoulder to stop him advancing.

'If we're as doomed as you say then why not tell us what's up there?' Granddad asked.

The troll didn't reply. He simply spat a big lump of pus onto the deck and looked out to sea.

'I've had enough of this!' Roared Arto, storming across the longship and grabbing the ropes around the troll in his powerful jaws. He lifted the squirming troll with ease and hung him over the side of the ship.

'Please don't kill me, don't kill me. I can't swim.' The troll pleaded.

'Even if you could swim it would be hard with those ropes around you. Don't you agree, Arto?' Granddad leant over the side of the ship and smiled at the terrified troll.

'Let's try one more time. What's in that forest?' Granddad asked.

'Ok, ok, I'll tell you. Put me down, put me down.' The troll howled.

Arto lifted the troll back on to the ship and dropped him heavily onto the deck.

'We're waiting.' Granddad said nodding to Arto, who roared.

'The tribes live in the forest,' the troll said, looking around as if he expected the Master to appear and strike him down for telling them.

'What tribes?' Elder Thomson asked.

'There are tribes in this world who don't follow the Master. They use some kind of magic to keep us out of the forests.'

The troll stopped talking and looked at his feet.

'How did they keep someone as powerful as the Master at bay?' Granddad asked.

'We don't understand their magic. The Master has been trying for as long as I can remember, but we've never broken any of their forest rings. If we get too close, we die.'

'So we would die if we tried to enter the forest?' George asked.

'Why don't you try and see?' the troll answered with a sneer.

'Has anyone ever gone in there who wasn't part of the tribes?' Granddad asked the troll.

Graff didn't answer; he looked at his feet and mumbled something into his chest. Arto roared and strode towards the troll.

'The time for games is over. Tell us or you go over the side.'

'There was one. Some years ago, a stranger was let into their world. We didn't know where they came from or who they were, but they took them in.'

The troll's voice came out as a whisper as if he was scared he would be heard by the wrong person.

'Maybe they'll let us in as well. It's a chance worth taking. If there are people in this place not with the Master then we need to try and get their help.' Granddad said.

Peter and George looked at each other, then to the forest. Both were worried about believing the troll, but at the same time, they could see Granddad's point. The ship grew quiet as they neared the shore.

*****

The Master watched the longship from the safety of the fog. There is no way they would follow her now. She turned and looked at the children. Both were clearly terrified and confused. Neither of them had uttered a word since they came through the portal. The boy would be a good slave; he looked strong enough. She had something else in mind for the girl, something else entirely.

She looked back at the longship as it changed course and headed for the shore.

'You were right Master. Graff is leading them towards the forest.' Tolldruck said, coming to stand and watch with the Master.

'Like I said to the Shifter, Graff has his uses. He'll tell them about the tribes if he hasn't already. He's probably even told them about her.' The Master smiled as she spoke.

She looked at Tolldruck's chest and could see the wound was starting to heal. Her Magic was working against the liquid sunshine burn.

'You need to be more careful. If the boy had hit you with more liquid sunshine, or whatever it was you said he used on the Shifter you would be dead. No amount of my magic could bring you back.'

'I know Master. I let anger cloud my judgement. It won't happen again. We need to be careful of the boy with the potions. Whatever that is in his left hand it's very powerful.' Tolldruck replied.

'They know more than we thought. They knew how to defeat the Shifter. We need to be careful, and not underestimate them again.' the Master said.

'Why don't we attack now?' Tolldruck asked.

'Not yet, like I said before, Graff has his uses. If he leads Jacob to the tribe, and they accept him they might help him come looking for these two. We could destroy that tribe, find out how they use their magic and kill Jacob all at the same time.' The Master smiled as she spoke.

'Please Master, leave Jacob to me. I want him to suffer.'

'You'll get your chance, but for now, we must get ready. One way or another they will come for the children and that will be their final mistake.'

The Master turned away and shouted orders at the trolls who started the boat moving. She had managed to get the Viking to her world, and all the advantages were with her.

Chapter 2

The longship stopped as near to the shore as possible. Granddad, his brothers, Arto and the boys got off and waded through the shallow water to the small stone beach. The Elders and Jake were to wait on the ship with the Vikings until they were sure it was safe.

'It's ok boy; I'll be back soon. You need to stay and guard the troll.' Peter had told him before turning and jumping into the shallow water.

When they were all on the beach, Granddad gathered them round.

'We have to be careful. There's something different about whoever is in there, but that doesn't mean they'll be friendly to us.' He said.

'There's only one way to find out.' Arto growled, then started walking towards the forest.

'I guess we follow him.' George said to Peter.

'I guess we do. I hope whoever lives here can help us find Charlotte and James.' Peter replied.

They followed the others up the hill towards the forest. The only sounds were their feet crunching on the dead earth. Peter looked around and wondered what could cause such destruction. Everywhere he looked the land was destroyed, scorched and lifeless. The only exception was the forest.

Suddenly there was movement ahead of them. A large group of children emerged from the forest, walked forward a few feet then stopped. The children reminded Peter of films he had seen of American Indians. They were dark skinned with dark hair, and their clothes were basic and made of light brown cloth.

The group continued to approach the children, finally stopping just a few feet from them. Granddad moved forward and began to speak.

'We mean you no harm, we've come to this world to search for two children that were stolen from our own.' He said.

'We know you mean no harm Jacob.' One of the older children replied.

The fact that they knew his name shocked Granddad. He looked to the others and could see they were all just as surprised.

'How do you know who I am?' Granddad asked.

'We know a great deal about you Viking. We're your friends, but we can't stay out of the forest it's not safe. You must follow us. There is someone who wants to see you. Your passage into the forest has been granted.'

The group exchanged puzzled looks, but what choice did they have. The children turned and walked towards the forest.

'How do they know who you are Granddad?' Peter asked.

'I've no idea Peter. I'm more interested in who wants to see me.' Granddad replied.

They followed the children into the forest. The children were talking in excited tones and kept glancing back at the group. They seemed more interested in Granddad and Arto than anyone else.

'Who do you think we're going to see?' George asked Peter.

'I don't know. I still can't work out how they knew who Granddad was.' Peter replied.

The children became excitable and began shouting and running ahead. They ran to keep up with them and soon found themselves in a small village. There were lots of wooden huts arranged in an orderly fashion. The huts formed small streets and, in the centre, there were several larger buildings all made of wood.

'This place is bigger than Campbell's Cove.' George said, which earned him a dig in the ribs from Peter.

As they neared the centre, several adults began to emerge from the huts. They smiled and nodded as the group walked by. It was almost like a welcoming committee. A door in the biggest hut opened and out stepped a large man. He had dark hair, skin and eyes and was dressed in the same manner as the children. He raised his hand and all the tribespeople stopped talking and stood silently.

'Welcome, Jacob and Arto. You and your companions are welcome here. While you are in this forest nothing can harm you. It's one of the only safe places left in our world,' the man said.

'Did he say his world? I thought this was the witches' world.' George whispered to Peter, who shrugged in response.

'Jacob, I ask that your friends stay here, and let my people take care of them. There is someone I would like you to talk to.' He beckoned for Granddad to come forward.

Granddad looked at the others then nodded and followed the man inside the main structure. The inside of the hut was impressive. There was a main corridor and going off that were five doors. Three doors on the right and two on the left. The floor had been covered with bark and vines ran along its timber walls. There were gaps in the wood that let in light and air, and Granddad could see several large stones that were covered in fire fungus.

'She's through the second door on your right. Please go in.' The man said, showing the way with one outstretched arm.

Granddad nodded and walked down the corridor. He paused briefly outside the door, his hand inches from the wooden handle. He looked back once at the man before pushing the door open.

'Oh my goodness...' Was all he could say as he stumbled involuntarily backwards against the wall.

'Hello Jacob, it's been a long time.' The woman said rising from her chair as tears ran down her cheeks.

*****

Peter and George were taken to a table off to the side of the main square of the village. Porr and Tofi sat with them, and Arto sat nearby. They were given fruit, bread and the best tasting juice George had ever had. He gulped down his cup and asked for more. Arto was brought two large fish which he ate in one bite. Porr and Tofi sat silently, and never took their eyes off the door that Granddad had gone through.

'What do you think's going on in there?' Peter asked George.

'I've no idea. I wonder who wants to meet him.' George replied. He looked around at the people who had been serving them and continued.

'Do you think they'll be able to help us find Charlotte and James?'

'I hope so if they can't our only hope is the troll.' Peter replied.

'That's not much hope at all. The troll may have guided us here, but I don't think he will take us to the Master so easily.' Arto said coming to sit next to them.

'Why not?' George asked.

'Would you want to be the one who led your enemies to the Master's door?' Arto said, answering George's question with one of his own.

Before they could discuss it any further Granddad reappeared at the door. He looked for the boys and when his eyes met Peter's he smiled.

'Peter, George come inside. There is someone I would like you to meet.'

The boys exchanged glances before walking over to where Granddad was. Peter went first with George falling behind as he finished off another cup of juice. They reached the door, and Granddad motioned for them to stop.

'The person you're about to meet is very special. This changes everything.' Granddad said.

'Granddad, have you been crying?' Peter asked looking at faint tear lines on Granddad's face.

'Maybe a little Peter, but there's no sadness here.' Granddad said turning around and ushering the boys after him.

They entered the room and sitting in a chair at the far side was a woman who looked vaguely familiar to Peter. She rose as she saw them come in and looked at both of them.

'This must be Peter. He has your eyes Jacob, and your height.' The woman said before turning her attention to George.

'George, I believe you've been a great help to Peter and his Granddad. For that, we are forever thankful.'

'I'm sorry, who are you?' George said looking from the woman to Granddad.

Peter looked at his Granddad then back to the woman. Where had he seen her before? Not her exactly, but someone who looked like her. Maybe her daughter or maybe it was an old photograph somewhere. Suddenly it dawned on him. He looked at Granddad who could see the understanding written all over Peter's face. Granddad smiled and nodded. Peter turned to George and said simply:

'She's my Gran.'

Far away from the little forest town, out in the ocean, the portal opened briefly. This went unnoticed by everyone on board the Viking ship. They were too busy awaiting news of their friends to see the brief flash of light caused by the opening. From that distance, they certainly wouldn't have noticed the beast coming through. It noticed them, though, it could sense them. It lifted its head out of the water and turned until it could see them. The Shifter smiled to himself. His enemies were close by, and he had a score to settle.

Chapter 3

'What do you mean your Gran? I thought your Gran had died before you were born?' George said looking from Peter to the lady.

'Melissa's body was never found. The boat was found shattered into a hundred pieces, but we never actually found her.' Granddad said. He kept looking at the woman as he spoke. He turned back to the boys and continued.

'I think it's best if Melissa tells you what she told me. Then you'll understand, and hopefully, this will make sense.' He sat down next to the boys as Melissa sat back in her chair and closed her eyes. She opened them and smiled at them all.

'I used to love taking trips out into the ocean. I would row my little boat out and sit listening to the water all around me. There was a peace to being out there alone. I knew to stay away from shipping lanes and keep clear of any passages into the pier at the beach.' The story had begun, and it struck Peter that his Gran was just as at home telling stories as his Granddad was.

'I knew that if I stayed close enough to the shore, the current wouldn't be strong enough to damage the boat or pull me further out. The night was still, and the sky was clear. The stars always look amazing on summer's nights in the Cove. I was looking up at the stars when there was a flash of light, and suddenly a large ship crashed onto the water right next to me.'

'The impact shattered my boat and sent me through the air. I landed in the water and frantically swam to the surface. When I opened my eyes, I couldn't believe it. There was no sign of the ship or my boat, save for a few pieces of shattered wood. The stars had vanished, and I was looking at the sky you saw when you arrived.' She paused and looked at Peter.

'I remember thoughts were racing through my mind. Where was I? How do I get back to my daughter? Your mother. I saw the shore and swam as fast as I could to get there. I finally reached land, exhausted and sore. I crawled onto the beach and blacked out. I woke up here, in this village.'

'What happened? Did you try and come back?' Peter asked feeling slightly foolish for asking such an obvious question.

'When I woke up several of the adults were sitting around me. They had wrapped me up to keep me warm. When I asked them where I was, they told me that this place, this world, is called Vultraha. This is their world, although it had been overrun by the witches and their hordes.'

'So, this isn't the witches' world?' George asked.

'No George, well not really. This world belongs to the tribes. Tribes like this one that I was lucky enough to be rescued by. The witches came from underground and began conquering and plundering every village and town they could find. Nobody knows how long they were down there or why they suddenly decided to attack.'

'Why haven't they taken this place?' Peter asked.

'This forest is guarded by a deep magic. The tribe that found me are the oldest on this planet. They have Elders, much like the ones in Campbell's Cove, who can cast spells that keep the evil away. The witches don't need this small part of the world to control the majority of it. They stopped trying to come in here some years back. Their losses were too great. There are several such places where other tribes still live. They keep a constant watch, though, looking for anyone who is foolish enough to stray too far from safety.'

'Couldn't you use a portal to come home?' George asked.

'The portals are something the witches create. We've no idea how they work. Leaving the forest places us in constant danger. We have scouts that go out and map the positions of our enemies. My only hope of ever returning to our world was if Jacob somehow came to this one. I still can't believe you're here,' she said, reaching out and taking Jacob's hand before continuing.

'The tribe will help you in any way they can to find your friends. Most of them will not leave this forest. It's not safe out there for anyone now.'

'We've left our friends on the longship. Will they be safe?' Jacob asked.

'We should go and get them. They will be safer here with us. There's a small inlet on the island that leads to a harbour. The harbour is protected by magic. The Master must know you followed her through the portal. She may be watching and waiting for a chance to strike.'

*****

The Elders sat on the longship constantly looking up at the forest hoping to see their friends returning.

'What do you think's happening?' Elder Sanderson asked.

'I'm not sure I just hope they can help us.' Elder Thomson replied.

'I don't like this, being out in the open. I mean, I just wish they would hurry up. The sooner we get back to our world the better.'

Jake was sleeping on Elder Sanderson's lap when the longship rocked ever so gently. The others barely noticed, but Jake raised his head and let out a small growl.

'Be quiet boy.' Elder Sanderson stroked Jake's head as he spoke.

'I wonder what that was about.' Elder Thomson said.

'Probably a bad dream or maybe he was just growling at him.' Elder Sanderson replied motioning towards Graff.

They both looked at the troll who was still in the same position but was smiling.

'What are you smiling at?' Elder Thomson asked.

'I don't think the dog had a bad dream, but you're about to live a real nightmare.' The troll replied. He smiled, exposing his rotten teeth and wart covered tongue.

The longship rocked again and this time, the Vikings were all up on their feet looking over the side of the ship. The Elders got up and took out their potions. They remembered Tolldruck's attack on the ship and looked fearfully at each other.

Without further warning, a monster burst from the water. It flew out of the foaming sea and landed on the deck. The Vikings drew their swords but kept their distance. Jake growled, backing away as he did. The beast stood up. Tall and powerful it towered above them all. Soulless white eyes stared out from a dark grey face. The impossibly large mouth broke into a smile as it savoured their fear. Taller than Tolldruck, and more terrifying in appearance the beast showed off razor sharp talons as it flexed its powerful hands open and shut.

The whole body was dark grey, and powerful. There were 5 gills on each side, level with the ribcage, and battle scars in several places. It stood staring at them, unmoving, seemingly willing one of them to make the first move.

The Vikings finally advanced as one unit. Twenty-five of them, with swords and shields raised, approached the monster. The creature charged into the Vikings with blurring speed, knocking several off their feet, but not killing any of them.

It attacked again, this time running into the centre of the Vikings, throwing them effortlessly through the air. Their swords were not quick enough to find their mark. The monster appeared to be toying with them. Several dazed and injured Vikings were getting back to their feet when Elder Sanderson panicked and threw a liquid sunshine bomb. The beast caught the bomb, plucking it out of mid-air as if it was plucking an apple from a tree. It appeared to crush the bomb until the light went out. The monster opened its hand revealing dark charcoaled remains. It wagged one finger at the Elders.

'How quickly you forget. Liquid sunshine can't kill me. Nothing can kill me.' The beast said smiling as it did.

'Shifter.' Elder Thomson's voice was full of alarm. He was unable to hide the surprise and fear.

'I thought you were dead.' Elder Sanderson's voice came out as a whisper.

'Fools, did you think I'd been defeated?' the Shifter said taking a step towards them.

'If you've come for the troll, take him and leave us alone.' Elder Thomson pointed at Graff as he spoke.

'Him? Why would I want him?' the Shifter said. He moved over to Graff and lifted him off the deck with ease. He dangled Graff upside down, studied him for a moment, and then let him drop back down on his head.

'I've no interest in Graff. You can keep him and do what you want with him. I want the boy.' The Shifter said the word boy with disdain and anger.

'Which boy?' Elder Thomson asked.

'The one who thought he'd killed me.' The Shifter replied.

'He's gone into the forest.' The shaky voice belonged to Graff. He was still slumped on the deck and was trying to sit up.

'He'll have to come out some time.' The Shifter said.

The Elders exchanged looks after the Shifter spoke. A silent understanding passed between them.

'Let's have some fun while we wait.' The Shifter continued before charging into the Vikings again.

This time, he wasn't fooling around. He picked two up as he ran through them. He crushed the life out of them with his bare hands and threw them into the sea. The Shifter roared and stretched his arms out wide.

The Vikings charged him as one. His speed was incredible as he dodged swords and shields landing his blows with ease. Viking after Viking fell, some dead and some dazed. The Shifter was too powerful. He seemed to relish the fight and didn't have a mark on him as half the Vikings lay unmoving on the deck.

Those that remained formed a shield around the Elders and Jake. The Shifter smiled then began walking forward.

He was taking his time, savouring their fear. He would finish off the Vikings first then toy with Elders before killing them too. He was about to attack when he noticed a change in the expressions on the Elders' faces. They were no longer looking at him and appeared to be looking above his head with confusion all over their faces.

The Shifter turned just as the first glowing arrow cut through his leg embedding itself deep into his thigh. His skin turned white around the wound. He roared with pain but did not have time to remove it as another three arrows crashed into him. Two hit his left arm, and one hit his shoulder. He roared again as he looked to where the arrows were coming from.

He could make out tribesmen running down the hillside. They stopped then fired off another volley. The Shifter was injured and couldn't move quickly enough to avoid them all. Two missed their marks, but the others hit home. He cried out in pain as three arrows ploughed into his stomach.

The Shifter stumbled to the side of the longship. He tried to steady himself, but his legs appeared to give way. He tipped over the side and landed heavily in the water. The Shifter sank from view as the Elders rushed over to watch.

They looked up to the shore and could see their friends running towards them. Arto led the way crashing down the hillside and across the beach. Black dust rose up all around the bear as he charged forward. Jake barked excitedly as Peter came closer.

They reached the ship, and Granddad and the boys climbed on board while the others stood guard on the shore. Jake ran to Peter and bounced around his legs. They looked at the fallen Vikings then to the Elders.

'What was it that attacked you?' Granddad asked.

Elder Thomson looked at them all, his eyes finally resting on George.

'It was the Shifter.' He said.

They all looked shocked.

'Wh-what do you mean? We saw him die. Arto smashed the Shifter into a thousand pieces.' George stumbled on every word.

'He's very much alive, and there's something else.' Elder Sanderson added.

'What is it?' Granddad asked putting his hand on George's shoulder.

'He seems even stronger here. He caught a liquid sunshine bomb and crushed the light and heat out of it. We watched as it turned to dust in his grip.'

'He did what?' Peter could hardly believe what he had been told.

'It's true, he just plucked it out of the air and crushed it.' Elder Thomson said looking to Granddad and making the motion with his hand as he spoke.

'We can discuss this later. For now, we need to move the Longship. There's a small harbour on the other side of the forest. It's protected, and we must move there now. If the Longship stays out in the open it won't last long.' Granddad replied.

Granddad asked them all to check the Vikings, and the Elders used their potions on any that could be saved. Eight Vikings had died during the attack. Granddad shook his head and looked to the sky.

'We should have stayed. We should have made sure everyone was safe before leaving the ship.' He said without looking at any of them.

'We weren't to know Granddad. We made the right choice. How were we to know the Shifter was still alive?' Peter replied.

Granddad looked at Peter and smiled sadly. He said no more and began organising the Vikings. He motioned to Arto on the shore who seemed to understand and turned to walk towards the forest again. The tribesmen followed on after Arto, seemingly satisfied that the danger had passed for now. Porr and Tofi leapt on to the longship and watched the water with their swords drawn.

'One thing I don't understand is why didn't the Shifter free him?' George asked, looking at Graff who was hunched against the side of the boat.

'We offered him to the Shifter in return for leaving us alone. The Shifter had no interest in him.' Elder Sanderson said.

'It seems you're all alone. We can't take you into the forest. The tribe would never allow you to enter.' Granddad said going over and sitting down next to Graff.

'What do we do with him then?' George asked. Half hoping the answer was to drop the troll overboard. He didn't trust him and felt uneasy around him even if he was tied up.

'We'll take him as far inland as we can then tie him to something. Fate can decide from there.' Granddad answered.

'What's to stop something coming and rescuing him?' Peter asked looking unsure of the plan.

'Peter, the Shifter could have freed him and chose not to. He doesn't appear to be of any importance to them, and now is of little use to us. He's a pathetic creature. However, I won't kill an unarmed and bound enemy, but I won't help him either.' Granddad replied looking at the troll.

'You can't just leave me tied to a tree.' Graff spoke in a voice full of defeat. He looked at them one by one then continued.

'I can take you right to the Master. The tribe might be able to show you the area to look in, but I can give you the exact place.' His voice had a pleading tone that was close to begging.

'Why would you do that?' Peter asked.

'He'd do it because he's scared. He has nowhere else to turn. His only hope is to get to the Master and hope she's more sympathetic to his plight than the Shifter was.' Granddad replied before Graff could give his answer.

The longship moved slowly around the island and finally they could see the small inlet which led to the harbour. There was barely room for the ship to make its way forwards. Tribesmen were gathered with their weapons drawn. They watched the longship come closer then without warning a horn was blown. The deep booming sound caused the Vikings to stop rowing and look to the tribesmen.

'What does it mean Granddad?' asked Peter, who was holding and stroking Jake.

'I'm not sure, but it sounded like a warning signal. I think maybe this is where we must leave our friend.' Granddad replied looking at the troll.

Granddad spoke to his brothers, and they approached Graff. Between them, they picked him up and threw him overboard. Graff landed heavily on the grass next to the water. Porr and Tofi followed the troll over the side and dragged him to a nearby tree. They freed his legs, but left his top half tied and secured him to the tree, ignoring his shouts of protest.

When Graff was securely tied Granddad looked to the tribesmen who beckoned them on.

'Looks like you were right. They didn't want that troll coming any closer.' Peter said.

The Longship docked in the harbour, and Granddad asked the Viking crew to stay on board. The Elders and

Jake joined the others, and together they all set off for the village in the forest.

Graff watched them go and cursed them. How dare they leave him tied to a tree like this? He looked around nervously. Every noise made him jump, and every gust of wind chilled him to the bone. He tried to free himself, but it was hopeless. The Vikings had tied him too tightly.

He was terrified; barclues roamed the area near to the forest. He doubted very much whether one of them would care what side he was on or that he wasn't a tribesman. He had just finished that thought when he heard the footsteps behind him.

Heavy footsteps crunched into the forest floor. The dead bark snapped and cracked with each one. Graff dared not move; he sat motionless with his eyes closed hoping that whatever this visitor was it would move on and leave him alone. Terror gripped him. Sweat began to run down his face.

Suddenly the noise stopped. Graff listened intently, but there was nothing. He opened his eyes and gave out a slight shriek as he found himself staring at Tolldruck.

'You are a pathetic waste of life Graff.' Tolldruck growled.

'How easy was it for them to capture you? Did you even put up a fight?' he continued.

'How could I? Everyone else had left, and it was just me against all of them.' Graff answered.

'Maybe if you had fought with your men rather than hiding you wouldn't have been left behind.' Tolldruck could not hide the contempt in his voice for the troll. He despised Graff, and if the Master had agreed he would have killed him right now.

'A-are you here to help m-me or k-kill me?' Graff asked in a quiet, shaky voice.

'If it was my choice, you would already be dead. The Master wants to see you. She will decide what happens to you.'

Without another word Tolldruck slashed the ropes with one powerful claw. He picked up Graff and shoved him roughly back through the dead forest.

Chapter 4

They arrived back at the village and were ushered into the house where Melissa was waiting. Granddad had filled the Elders in on the walk back. They were both amazed to know she was alive. When they saw her, they embraced like the old friends they were.

'I can't believe it's you.' Elder Thomson said.

'It's me; I've been waiting for this day for a very long time.' Melissa replied.

She said hello to Elder Sanderson and gave him a hug.

'We have work to do, and we believe we know where the Master will take the children. This is Mirka, he is the head scout here, and knows the land better than anyone.' Melissa said, pointing to a tribesman who was sitting at a table off to the side of the room.

Mirka stood up and walked over to them. He shook hands with Granddad and the Elders and nodded at the boys.

'The Master and her hordes control most of this world as Melissa has already told you. There are several places that they could take the children, but one is more likely than any others.' Mirka unfolded a large hand drawn map and placed it on the centre table before continuing.

'When the Master first arrived here her army struck fast and captured the main city. We had never been attacked before and had never used our magic to defend ourselves. This had been a peaceful world. Our naivety and the speed of the attack meant the city fell quickly. Hundreds of our people died, and the rest fled to places like this forest.' Mirka ushered them all to gather round the map before continuing.

'This is the forest where we are now. The main city was here.' He said pointing to an area not far from where they were.

'Why would the Master take them there?' Granddad asked.

'She wouldn't, not to the city itself, but below it. They came up through the centre of the city. It was like the ground just vanished, and thousands of trolls and goblins spilled into our world. We have since discovered that there's a huge cave system under the city. I believe this is where your friends will be taken; if she keeps them alive.'

'What do you mean if she's keeping them alive?' George's voice sounded shaky and uncertain when he asked the question.

'What I mean is if she was using the children to get you to follow her here, she might have no more use for them.' Mirka replied.

The words hung in the air between them all. It was something neither Peter, nor George had considered.

'I'm sure they're alive boys, but we need to move quickly to get them back home.' Granddad said trying to reassure them.

'How do we get to them if it's dangerous to leave the forest?' Elder Thomson asked.

'It'll be dangerous, and there's no guarantee of success, but if your friends are to have any chance then all we can do is try.' Mirka replied.

'What kind of enemy will we face out there?' Granddad asked.

'There are the usual trolls and goblins which can be easily defeated or avoided, however, there are other things out there that are much more dangerous. You've met the Shifter and Tolldruck, so you know how dangerous they can be.'

'The Shifter seems stronger here.' Elder Sanderson said, then explained what happened on the ship.

'They have done something to our world. The sky was not always the colour you see today. There is a strange glow that can be seen coming from the centre of the city. We believe it comes from the place the ground fell in. When that glow appeared, the sky began to change very slowly. The air we breathe began to change. It's difficult to explain, but it's like they have changed our world to suit their needs; as if being on the surface doesn't suit them or isn't natural to them.' Mirka looked to each of them to see if they understood.

'What do you think they did?' Peter asked.

'We believe that whatever is in the city gives them life or feeds them in some way. Maybe the closer they are to it the stronger they are. That could be why the Shifter seemed stronger here.' Mirka replied.

'If that's true then we can find whatever's causing it and stop it.' George said.

They all looked at George and Granddad smiled.

'Let's concentrate on finding Charlotte and James. Once they are safe, we can maybe look into that.' Granddad looked at George and nodded his head before continuing.

'Mirka, tell us everything you can about the caves and what we must cross to get there.'

They all gathered round as Mirka began to describe what lay between them and the Master.

'Once your feet touch the scorched earth outside of this safe area you're no longer protected by our magic. They seem to know when one of us leaves and within a few minutes, we can hear their trolls and goblins looking for us. They are stupid, and easily evaded, however, a larger group might have to stand and fight rather than hide.' He looked at them as he spoke studying their faces for a reaction.

'Occasionally they will send a barclue with them. These are wild beasts with massive jaws, powerful arms, but some strangely human traits as well. They've ragged brown fur, and their only instinct appears to be to attack as soon as they see an enemy. They are not very intelligent, but they are incredibly strong and fast.'

'Granddad that sounds like the creature you described when you told us about the portal in the forest.' Peter said.

'You're right Peter.' replied Granddad, before quickly telling Mirka about his encounter.

'You had a lucky escape, Jacob. Not many people see a barclue up close and survive.' Mirka reached for another map and unrolled it before continuing.

'Once we leave the forest there's a river to cross. There are options open to us, but none are very welcoming. We can use boats to cross, but this will give the enemy advanced warning that we are coming. We could cross at Travellers' Pass, which is a bridge built by our people. It's safe and strong and has been left intact by the Master.'

'If they've left it intact, we have to assume they use it, and that it will be guarded.' Granddad stated.

'That's correct Jacob. Which leaves us with one option; the cave system of Mantrutha. The caves go under the river and come out on the south edge of the city. I've been through them many times as have most of our scouts. It's been a while since I was in them so I've no idea what's there now.' Mirka looked at Jacob.

'Wait, I thought you said that the Master and her armies came up out of caves?' Peter asked.

'They did, however, the Mantrutha caves are a separate system, not linked to the ones below the city.' Mirka replied.

'The caves do seem to offer us the best chance of getting there without being caught.' Granddad said looking to the others for agreement.

'Why does it always have to be caves?' George asked.

Granddad laughed, and Peter nudged George. The decision had been made. They would go via the caves if they got that far.

*****

The Master could see the fear in the faces of James and Charlotte. She smiled as she approached them.

'Don't worry, if I had wanted you dead, it would have happened already. You two have proved extremely useful. Without you, we wouldn't have been able to lure Jacob to this world.'

'What will you do with us?' James asked.

'Your reward for being excellent bait will be to serve me for the rest of your life. Which, believe me, will be longer than you think.'

The Master smiled as she looked at both of them. She could see the tears running down Charlotte's cheeks.

'You shouldn't cry. Your fate is something else entirely. A lot more appealing than Jacob's and the boys.' When they come for you, and they will come for you, we will be waiting. There are worse things than the Shifter in this place; things that prefer the shadows, creatures that will not take kindly to strangers coming into their territory.'

Before the Master could say anymore, the boat stopped moving. They had arrived at a large dock on the outskirts of a primitive looking city. The city was surrounded by a huge wooden wall with large gates that sat open near the dock. The dock itself was lined with trolls and goblins all standing perfectly still. Suddenly the Master was shouting orders, and the dock exploded into life.

The children were carried in their cages up through the city. Charlotte looked into the faces of the trolls and goblins as they passed by. Some smiled and licked their lips as they passed. She heard one ask if they were dinner, and another ask he if could just eat an arm or a leg. She tried to block out the noise, and the faces, and her thoughts turned to Peter and George. She knew they were here, in this terrible place, somewhere. Would they be able to save them, what did the Master mean when she said there were worse things than the Shifter? After being close to the Shifter, Charlotte found it hard to imagine anything worse.

They travelled over dirt streets that had been cut through what was once a forest. There were houses dotted here and there, small wooden huts mainly. The number of houses increased, and Charlotte got the sense that this had once been a busy city. The dirt roads looked well used, and the houses and other buildings must have held hundreds, if not thousands, of people at one point.

'Where have they all gone?' she asked herself.

'Most of them are dead. Some have scattered into the protected forests.' The Master appeared next to Charlotte's cage and answered her unasked question.

'This was once their main city. For years we waited until the time was right. They were so confident and foolish. We lived below them and around them for years, and they never knew. We were a fairy tale you tell your children; a warning to do as you're told. The thing is Charlotte; some fairy tales are real.' The Master smiled, said no more, and moved past Charlotte up to the head of the line.

She read my mind. It was all Charlotte could think. She was sure she hadn't spoken any words and yet the

Master answered her question. She looked at James and wondered what he was thinking. She hoped it wasn't anything that could help the Master. The next time they were alone she had to tell him.

Suddenly the line stopped. Charlotte looked ahead and could see they were standing next to a huge hole in the centre of the city. A glowing light was coming directly out of the hole. The strange purple glow was going right up into the sky. The more she looked, the more she was sure it was actually like a stream of light shooting upwards. There seemed to be a strange flow to it. It was like watching a waterfall in reverse. She looked up to the sky and could see the light spread out and give the sky its colour.

Charlotte looked over at James who was now staring at the sky as well. Now and then a small burst of darker purple shot up the stream and vanished into the sky.

She felt the jolt of the cage being lifted as they were carried forward towards the hole. She could see a walkway had been built that appeared to go deep underground. There were four watch towers around the hole, and she saw trolls standing on each one looking out at the city. The Master spoke to some of the trolls who remained above ground while the cages were carried past them. Down into the hole they went. The walkway wound around the strange light. At times Charlotte was so close she could have reached out and touched it. Something inside told her not to; there was something about that stream of light that scared her.

From their position in the cages, neither James nor Charlotte could see where the light was coming from. It was mesmerising to watch the flow. There was no sound, and the only change was when one of the dark purple balls of light shot up.

Further and further down they went until they reached the bottom of the hole. Charlotte looked up and was amazed at how far down they had travelled. The mouth of the hole seemed far away. Is this where these things come from? Charlotte looked at James and saw the look on his face. His mouth was open, and his eyes were wide. Charlotte followed his gaze and then she saw it, the source of the light. She couldn't believe her eyes; this couldn't be real.

There in front of them was a huge cauldron. The stream of light shot up from it into the air above them. Every few seconds the cauldron bubbled, and a darker purple pulse shot up the beam of light into the sky.

'Impressive, isn't it?' The Master asked the question but didn't wait for an answer.

'This is just the very tip. Maybe I'll explain how it works later. For now, it's time for you two to see your room.' The Master smiled as she said this, and two trolls began to laugh.

To their surprise both James and Charlotte were taken out of their cages and marched away from the light. They walked deep into the caves before they came to a wooden door. One of the trolls opened the heavy old door, and they were pushed inside. The door slammed shut, and James and Charlotte took in their surroundings. They were in a small room that looked like it had been cut out of the rock. The floor and walls were made of a soft white stone while the ceiling was covered in a brightly coloured fungus.

Charlotte sat on the floor next to her brother and looked at him.

'Do you think they'll come for us?' she asked him.

'I hope so, the Master seemed to think they would,' James replied. 'I hope she was right, and I hope that whoever Jacob is, he can beat her and take us home.'

'I think she can hear our thoughts,' Charlotte said.

'What makes you think that?' James replied.

Charlotte told James what had happened earlier. James looked worried as he tried to think about what he had been thinking earlier. He didn't know where Peter and the others were, so he was sure he had no useful information. Still, the thought that the Master could read minds scared him.

'What do you think she meant when she said this is just the tip?' James asked.

'I don't know, there's so much we don't know.' Charlotte replied.

They huddled together, listening to the silence, trying to stay brave and strong for each other. All they could do now was wait and pray for rescue.

Chapter 5

'We must leave now! How can we wait when we know James and Charlotte need us?' Peter strode around the room agitated as he talked.

'Trolls and goblins can see very well in the dark. If we go now, we're only playing into their hands.' Mirka answered.

'He's right Peter, we wait until dawn and then we move. I don't think harm will come to your friends. The Master wants us, and she knows the only thing keeping us here is James and Charlotte.' Granddad intervened, trying to calm Peter down.

'I just feel we should be doing something. We've no idea where they are. We're assuming Mirka is right, but we don't know he is.' Peter stared at his Granddad waiting for his response.

'Peter, I believe that the Master will take them somewhere that's known to the tribes. She wants us to follow.'

'So why not let us follow when we came through the portal?' George asked, joining the conversation.

'The Master isn't stupid. A fight with us at that point is a fight she could easily lose. She's putting the odds in her favour. She believes she'll be in a stronger position if we have had to travel through danger to reach her. Maybe she's hoping not all of us make it, or that our strength is sapped by the journey.' Granddad's reply was sensible, and both boys could see it.

'I just feel helpless.' Peter said slumping onto the ground with his knees bent up to his chin.

'I know Peter, but your friends are relying on us to save them. Going in with haste is more likely to result in failure. We will rescue them and stop the Master.' Granddad looked into Peter's eyes as he spoke.

The door to the room opened, and two men came in; neither had the look of a warrior or a scout.

'My name is Jeron, and this is Baden.' The taller one said, pointing to his friend. They walked forward into the room, and he continued.

'We are the Elders for this tribe and would like to help you in any way we can.'

Elders Thomson and Sanderson stood up and introduced themselves. They talked about the potions they had brought, and they showed the tribal Elders their liquid sunshine. They explained what had happened with the Shifter, both in the Cove and here in this world. Elder Sanderson motioned for George to join them and showed the others the sunshine shooter.

'Excellent design, it's controlled by the wearer's arm movements?' Baden asked.

'Yes, it is, one side is liquid sunshine, and the other is liquid nitrogen.' Elder Sanderson replied.

'You say that your liquid sunshine bomb had no effect on the Shifter here?' Jeron said.

'That's right; he just plucked it out the air and crushed it.' Elder Thomson said, making the motion with his hand as he spoke.

'They must be stronger here; it could have something to do with that light that comes out of the city. Your potions will work fine against trolls and goblins, but the larger enemies might be a problem.'

'We do have something that can help, though. You saw the arrows that the Shifter was shot with when he was on the longship?' Baden asked.

'Yes we did, I was going to ask about that. What was on those arrows?' Elder Sanderson asked.

'If you'd like to come with us, we'll show you.' Baden answered.

The Elders looked to Granddad who nodded his head. They gathered up their things and headed for the door.

'George, I'd like you to come as well.' Baden said motioning to him to follow. 'I've something that might prove highly effective in that sunshine shooter of yours.'

George followed along as the Elders moved through the small town to what could only be described as a shack. George stood and looked at the building.

'Is this where you live?' he asked, looking dubiously at the shack.

'Yes, why?' Baden asked.

'It looks like a strong breeze could blow it over.' George replied.

'He does have a point. Are you sure it's safe?' Elder Thomson asked.

'It's what's inside that counts.' Jeron said before opening the door.

They all entered the small hut, and George doubted that they would all fit. He soon realised how wrong he was. The shack was just an entrance. As soon as you were inside you could see a staircase had been cut into the ground.

The stairs spiralled out of sight, lit by fire fungus. The tribal Elders led the way down and through a small corridor with a door at the end. They opened the door and inside there was a large oval shaped room.

In the room were several tables covered in mixing bowls which were all filled with various liquids. There were tables with bottles and weapons laid out and two hammock style beds in the corner.

Elder Thomson nudged Elder Sanderson and pointed to a table at the far side that was covered in arrows. Some had a dark grey colour to their tip. The tips shone in the soft light of the fire fungus.

'Are those the same as the arrows the tribe used against the Shifter?' Elder Sanderson asked.

'Yes, they are.' Baden replied walking over to the arrows.

'What are they made of?' George asked as he approached the table.

'A mixture of melted down metal infused with fire fungus.' Baden answered. He picked up an arrowhead that had not been attached and threw it to George.

George held it up to the light and turned it over in his hands.

'Where do you get the metal to make these?'

'From anywhere we can. The most common place is from the weapons of dead trolls and goblins.' Jeron said.

'Why do you make them? How did you know they would be effective against the Shifter?' George asked the question as he passed the arrowhead to Elder Sanderson.

'We weren't looking for something that could hurt or kill the Shifter. We were looking for something that could kill a barclue. Our usual arrows could kill trolls and goblins with ease. However, they made little or no impression on a barclue.' Baden picked up a couple of normal arrowheads and passed them around before continuing.

'We tried using their weapons on the barclues. The swords and axes could cause damage but close up combat against them almost always results in death. We had to come up with a way of using the metal without getting close. So, we began melting it down and forming arrowheads.'

'Could you not just stay out of their way? Stay in here where it's safe?' George asked.

'We can't. The protected area provides some food, but we have to go further afield for meat and the small inlet rarely has fish in it, so we have to go further out to fish. This means sending a hunting party with soldiers to protect them.' Baden replied.

'They know we are here, and they wait until a group leaves and then attack. We've no choice; our survival depends on the bravery of those that go outside the protected zone. Usually, it's just a few trolls or goblins that are quite stupid and easily defeated. However, when a barclue comes there's great danger.' Jeron added.

'We knew that the metal could hurt them and figured that if we could use it with our arrows, we would do more damage.' Baden said.

'Why do you use fire fungus with it?' Elder Thomson asked.

'Fire fungus reacts with the minerals in materials; it's how it feeds, and how it lights up. We heat the metal until its liquid then drop fire fungus in. When the metal cools the fungus fuses with it. When the arrowhead strikes, a target small cracks are formed in the metal. This allows the fire fungus to seep out and then it does what it always does. It looks for food.' Baden could see the Elders were beginning to understand.

'The fungus eats the barclues from the inside?' Elder Sanderson asked.

'That's correct. The fire fungus looks for minerals to use up and finds everything it needs in the blood and organs of a barclue or any other creature for that matter. It's fascinating really. You can hold fire fungus in your hand, and it will be quite harmless. It might even try and move away. Outside your body, it recognises you as the predator. Get it inside a body and it reacts completely differently.' Baden smiled as he finished, clearly proud of his design.

'That's amazing. So that's what was happening to the Shifter?' Elder Sanderson asked.

'Yes, it was. The Shifter is strong and can change every part of his being so I doubt it will kill him, but at least it slows him down. Now if we could get those arrow heads loaded into that the machine of yours, George, we would have one extraordinarily strong weapon.' Baden looked at George as he spoke.

George looked at the sunshine shooter and smiled. 'Let's get started.'

Back at the house Peter sat with his Granddad. He stared across at his Gran who was holding Jake and talking with Mirka

'How are you going to tell mum?'

'I've no idea Peter. We'll need to think of something. I lost your Gran for a very long time; I don't intend to lose her again.'

'It's so strange, I only ever heard about her or saw old photos. It's amazing that she's here with us now.'

'I can't imagine what she must have gone through. Being unable to get back and knowing we would all be missing her.' Granddad replied.

Peter's Gran came over to join them and handed Jake to Peter.

'Mirka and a few others will go with you. They know the way, and it will be safer for you.'

'Are you coming?' asked Peter.

'No Peter. An old lady would not be much use. I'll wait here for you.'

'Are you coming back with us?' he asked.

'Of course I am, Peter. I know it will be difficult, and there will be some explaining to do, but I want to go back to my family. I knew Jacob would come one day. I didn't know how or when, but I knew in my heart that he would come.'

'Mum will be so happy. She misses you and talks about you all the time.'

'I miss her too Peter. Now you have to promise me that you will bring your friends back so we can all go home.'

'I promise Gran; I'll do everything I can.'

Peter's Gran looked at him and smiled. 'Tell me about your life. Tell me who my Grandson is.'

Peter didn't know where to start. He was going to say that he was nothing remarkable. He was just a normal boy living a normal life, which would have been true if the same question had been asked ten days ago. Now, though, everything was different.

He told his Gran about school and his friends. How he had done well at sports and was doing well in class. He could see pride all over her face. He told her about spending two weeks every summer with his Granddad. He talked about his mum and dad and Jake.

'All of a sudden everything has changed. Suddenly I'm not just Peter, the boy who comes to Campbell's Cove for two weeks every summer. Now I'm the Grandson of a Viking who fights witches.'

'The circumstances have changed, Peter. It will take time to adjust and adapt, but you are still the same boy you've always been. None of us can escape our destiny.' His Gran answered.

'Was it part of your destiny to end up trapped in this world?'

'I believe it was. The reason has not yet been shown to me, but I think everything happens just as and when it's supposed to.'

'It's hard to believe that I'm to take over from Granddad. That one day it'll be me standing in his shoes.'

'Many things happen in life Peter, granted not all are as huge and unexpected as what has happened to you. Jacob tells me that you've coped very well and have proved yourself as a warrior on more than one occasion.' His Gran took his hand and continued. 'When the time comes for you to lead the battle against the Master or any other threat to this world, you will be ready, and you will succeed. I believe it in my heart, and so does Jacob.'

'Melissa is right Peter, both you and George have shown tremendous courage and skill already. When the time comes the world will be safe with you as a guardian.' Granddad said.

Just then George returned and once again had a huge smile on his face.

'Haven't we done this before?' Peter asked.

'Not like this we haven't.' Replied George still smiling.

He lifted his arms and Peter could see the familiar blue glow of the liquid nitrogen. The other side looked different, though. The liquid sunshine had gone, and it seemed like the shooter had been modified. Jake barked and danced around George's legs pleased to see him back.

'What's that?' Peter asked scooping Jake up and stroking his head.

'That's our new weapon against the Shifter and Tolldruck.' George replied.

George explained what the tribal Elders had told them about the arrowheads. The shooter had been altered to fit the arrows, and all George had to do was extend his arm in the correct way, and the arrowheads would be released.

'That's fantastic; they think you can bring down the Shifter and Tolldruck?' Peter asked.

'Well, they said it probably wouldn't kill the Shifter, but it will weaken him. Baden thinks if we can get enough fire fungus inside him it might mean he'll never regain his strength.' George replied.

Granddad looked concerned and studied the shooter for a couple of minutes.

'There is, once again, a lot of responsibility on your shoulders George.' He said.

'Where are the Elders?' Peter asked.

'They're altering their liquid sunshine bombs. They're working with Baden and Jeron to make them stronger.' George replied.

They talked for a while longer and then the boys were shown to another room which had basic beds in it. They were urged to try and sleep as tomorrow would be a tough day for all of them. Jacob went outside to find Arto. He finally found the large bear at the edge of the forest, looking out past the sea at the distant glow of the strange light.

'What's on your mind old friend?' Jacob asked.

'I keep thinking about that light. What does it do? How does it help them?'

'Maybe we'll find out very soon. If it does help them as Mirka thinks, then George was right. We need to shut it off.' Jacob replied looking out at the distant glow.

'It all looks so peaceful just now. Something tells me that tomorrow will change that.' Arto said, still staring at the light as it pulsed now and then.

'Tomorrow is going to be a hard day for all of us. Come on let's head back and get some rest. I think we'll need it.'

With that, Jacob and Arto turned and walked back to the small village in silence.

The Shifter watched the bear and the Viking talking. He got as close as he could and listened to their conversation. He willed just one of them to take a step outside the protected area. He would love to kill either of them right now.

His wounds from the arrows had begun to heal. The fire fungus hurt more than anything he had ever felt before. It slowed him down and made him weak, but only for a short time. He had been attacked with those arrows three times and each time his recovery was quicker. His body was learning to defend itself against the fungus. The fools had no idea what they were dealing with. It would seem that they would never understand that he couldn't be killed.

He watched as the two turned and walked back into the forest. Tomorrow they would come looking for the children. Tomorrow, he would crush them and anyone who tried to get in his way.

Chapter 6

Peter was woken from his dream by his Granddad shaking him.

'It's time to go, Peter.' His Granddad said before moving over to George and waking him as well.

'Come and meet us outside in five minutes.' Granddad said then turned and left the room.

George stretched and looked across to Peter. Peter was sitting on the edge of his bed letting the last clutches of sleep leave him. Jake was lying on his side with his tail wagging. Peter reached over and rubbed the dog's stomach.

'You know Peter I've been thinking about things,' George said as he stood up and began re-attaching the sunshine shooter.

'What have you been thinking?' Peter asked.

'I was thinking that when you take a friend on holiday, you make sure it's unforgettable.' George smiled, and Peter laughed as the two friends got up and went to join the others.

They walked outside and could see the sun was already up and trying to fight its way through the trees. They saw Porr, Tofi and Arto talking together next to a larger group. Granddad was part of the larger group as were all four Elders, Mirka and three other tribespeople.

'Boys, come and say hello.' Granddad said ushering them over.

'You know Mirka, and these are his best soldiers.' He continued.

Peter looked at the two men and one girl. The girl didn't look much older than him.

'Boys, go and eat something and then we'll set off.' Granddad said.

'Is this everyone that's going?' George asked.

'Yes, it is.' Mirka replied.

'What about the Vikings on the Longship?' George continued.

'George, we need those men to stay safe. When the time comes to leave, we need a crew capable of getting us home. With those we lost to the Shifter we can't afford to lose any more.' Granddad replied.

'I didn't think of that.' George sounded a bit sheepish when he spoke.

Peter and George went over to the large tables that they had sat at yesterday. Jake followed close behind hoping he was also going to be fed. The boys sat down and looked at all the food in front of them. There were several types of bread and lots of fruit and fish. George found the juice he had enjoyed yesterday and gulped down two large cups. They ate some fruit and bread, and Peter threw Jake a couple of small fish which he caught in mid-air and wagged his tail as he ate them.

Peter's Gran came out of her house and walked over to the boys. She picked up some fruit, poured a juice and sat across from them.

'How are you feeling boys, did you sleep well?'

'I slept very well, those beds are great,' George replied.

'Yes, they are extremely comfortable. How about you Peter?'

'I slept fine, it took me some time to drop off, though,' Peter replied.

'Worried about today?' his Gran asked.

'Yes, I am. We have to get them back. None of my friends would be in danger if it weren't for me.'

'That's not true Peter if you hadn't helped your Granddad stop the Master then all the children of the Cove would've been lost. Your friends would have never been found. As for George, it's true you brought him here but remember what I said about destiny Peter. George came with you and has played his part in stopping the Master and her army.'

Peter looked at George who smiled and made a gesture with his arms which showed off the sunshine shooter.

'We're a team, Peter. You need me here to keep you safe.' George said with his mouth full of breadcrumbs, and one large chunk escaped his mouth and was quickly eaten by Jake.

'Boys you must look after each other. You two form a strong team, and as you grow and learn you will become stronger. The warrior and the boy Elder.' Peter's Gran smiled when she said the last part.

'We need to work on my name, Peter's is much cooler.' George said with a smile.

'Gran, who's the girl in that group?' Peter asked.

Melissa looked over and saw who Peter was talking about.

'That's Zyanya. She might be young and small but trust me she can do some pretty amazing things when she needs to.'

'What kind of things?' George asked.

'Each person who Mirka has chosen to go with you has a great talent. Zyanya's talent is one that will come in very useful to you all.'

She smiled but said no more. Peter was about to ask his Gran to tell them more when his Granddad and Arto walked over.

'It's time to go boys. Come and join the group and get ready.' Arto said motioning with his head.

Peter hugged his Gran and picked up Jake. He gave his dog a hug and let Jake lick his face. Jake was staying behind with Gran. This was just too dangerous for a small dog.

'This time, do as you're told and stay here.' Peter said as he handed Jake over.

The boys and Arto joined the others while Jacob stayed back to talk to Melissa. Peter watched them talking for minute. They looked in his direction. His Granddad nodded then they hugged and parted.

'It's time to find your friends.' Granddad said as he re-joined the group. With that, they turned and followed Mirka towards the edge of the protected zone. Granddad wanted to walk by the Longship to tell the Vikings what was happening.

When they arrived, they found the Vikings on the shore being looked after by some of the tribespeople. Granddad went over and spoke to them with his brothers while the others waited nearby. Peter looked over at Zyanya who caught him staring and smiled. Peter blushed and turned away.

'Not very smooth for a great Viking warrior.' George whispered, earning him a kick from Peter.

Granddad and his brothers re-joined the group, and they began to walk further into the forest. Granddad stopped and together with Porr they went to a tree not far from the water. Peter could see the ropes that had held the troll were torn to pieces. There was no sign of Graff or whatever had freed him. Peter looked around at the scorched dead trees and earth and, not for the first time, felt the tingle of fear run down his spine.

*****

'It's good to see you again Graff. Tell me, how exactly did they catch you?' The Master watched Graff squirm as she asked the question. Tolldruck stood behind her, smiling at the troll's obvious discomfort.

'My men fled when the large bear attacked in the caves. I was left alone Master, if I hadn't hidden, I would have been killed. I was trying to get back outside when that awful dog attacked me. I was going to kill it, but the boy and his friends found me before I got the chance.' Graff couldn't look at the Master as he spoke.

'So, you watched your men die and then you were outsmarted by a dog and a boy?' The Master had a mocking tone in her voice.

'My men panicked and died before I could do anything. The dog got lucky.' Graff replied.

'You don't have to explain any further Graff. I was counting on your cowardice and instinct for survival. If it weren't for you, Jacob wouldn't have been able to follow me so easily.'

Graff didn't know how to take that statement, so he half smiled while almost making eye contact with the Master.

'They're going to come for the children today Graff. I want you to take a group of trolls and goblins and stop them. Your men are waiting for you at the edge of the city. Oh, and Graff, two barclues will be going with you.'

Graff looked frightened by the mention of the barclues. They were hard to control and had been known to attack and kill trolls if they got bored or hungry.

'Master, barclues could cause more problems than our enemies. You know they can attack goblins and trolls without thinking.' Graff said.

'Graff, barclues will only attack if you try and run away. They sense the change in your mood. If you're not fighting with them, then you're an enemy. As long as you don't get scared and run away, you'll be fine.' The Master smiled as she said this.

Graff gulped down hard as a large drop of sweat moved down his hideous face and ran off the end of his crooked nose.

'There's no more time for discussion Graff. Go and meet your men and bring an end to Jacob and his friends.' The Master dismissed Graff, who knew better than to try and argue any further.

Tolldruck watched as Graff made his way up towards the surface.

'Do you think he can stop Jacob?' he asked.

'Of course not, but it's time that Graff was put into a fight he can't run away from. He's served his purpose, and is of no more use to us.' the Master replied. She looked at Tolldruck and continued. 'Is there any word on the Shifter?'

'No Master he has not been seen.'

'He's somewhere nearby. The fact that he hasn't come to join us worries me. He could be planning something of his own. I think it was a mistake to involve him.'

'You did what you thought was right Master. He played his part in getting Jacob here, but it might have been better for us all if the boy had managed to kill him in the caves.' Tolldruck replied.

'You might be right old friend. However, you must find him, and bring him here. I don't want him killing Jacob before my plan is complete.'

'I'll find him, what will you do with the children?'

'The boy can die or become a slave. He doesn't interest me at all. I have plans for the girl, though.'

'What plans?' Tolldruck asked.

'I had two sisters. Two sisters that Jacob took from me, and I had a daughter once. It would be nice to have family again.' The Master said no more and turned around. Walking away with her back to Tolldruck she continued.

'Find the Shifter and bring him here. When he sees what I've planned, he won't want to miss it.'

Tolldruck watched the Master leave then turned and went the other way. He had to find the Shifter, and quickly.

The Master walked to where James and Charlotte were being held. She looked at the two goblins that were guarding the door; both were fast asleep. She shook her head and moved her hand first to the right then to the left. Both goblins flew through the air and landed heavily on the cave floor. They woke up, startled and alarmed. They drew their daggers and looked for what had attacked them. The goblins saw the Master at the same time and fell to their knees with their heads bowed.

'Forgive us, Master.' Said the one that had been tossed to the right.

'If you fall asleep again while you are guarding this door, I will personally feed you to a barclue or maybe I'll feed you to something much worse.' The Master offered no explanation as to what could be worse than a barclue.

The two goblins continued to apologise with their heads bowed and shuffled forward on their knees. The Master looked at them and shook her head. She moved her left hand across the door, and it sprung open.

James and Charlotte had heard the commotion and when the door burst open James put himself between his sister and the Master.

'How touching.' The Master said.

With one movement of her hand, James was thrown against the wall and pinned there. He was held, unable to move, two feet off the ground.

'We all try to protect our sisters James. I admire that about you. I tried to protect mine, but Jacob killed them anyway.'

'If you hurt her, I'll kill you.' James said through gritted teeth.

'I hardly think you're in a position to be issuing threats, James, do you?' the Master said looking into his eyes.

'I swear I'll kill you if you hurt her.' James repeated.

'Foolish boy trying to be the hero. You have courage James, and you should hold on to that.' The Master turned her attention to Charlotte.

'It's time for you to leave this prison cell. I'm not going to hurt you, Charlotte.'

'What do you want from me?' Charlotte asked with a trembling voice.

'I've something to show you.'

'What about James?'

'He can stay here for now.' The Master replied.

'I'm not leaving here without him.' Charlotte said trying to sound strong.

'That's a choice you don't get to make.' The Master said no more and with one flick of her hand, Charlotte was through the door.

The grip on James was released, and he ran to the door just a second too late. It slammed shut separating him from Charlotte.

Chapter 7

They had been walking for about an hour, and the forest was quiet. They had come to a clearing that was taking them towards a sloping hill. The dirt that covered the hill was black and dark grey almost like ash. Peter could see the ground dropping away in the distance and guessed they must be getting nearer to the water.

All that Peter could hear was the sound of their footsteps. When he listened harder and paid more attention, he realised that Mirka and the other tribespeople made no sound at all. He motioned to George first pointing to his ear then their feet. George gave Peter a puzzled expression and shrugged his shoulders.

'Look at their feet.' Peter whispered. 'They don't make any sound.' He continued.

George realised Peter was right and then noticed the tribespeople, including Zyanya, looking at them both with scornful faces.

'I think we're making too much noise.' George said before being quiet.

Peter looked over at Zyanya who shook her head twice then turned away. Another great move Peter thought to himself. He looked at his own feet, and his thoughts turned to James and Charlotte. He hoped they were ok and had not been hurt.

A chill-inducing roar snapped Peter out of his thoughts. The tribespeople all stopped moving, and everyone else followed suit. Mirka began climbing a tree, and the other tribespeople drew their weapons. Porr and Tofi drew their swords and backed up next to Peter and George. Granddad urged the Elders to get behind the Vikings. Arto stood at the front; his head held high sniffing the air.

The roar came again, this time from somewhere much closer. Within seconds Mirka appeared from the tree he had climbed. With one leap he landed perfectly balanced on the forest floor. Without missing a beat, he ran towards them.

'Lots of trolls and goblins are coming this way. They have two barclues with them.'

'What do we do?' George asked. The mighty roar sounded, and now they could hear the horrible voices of goblins and trolls.

'We could hide, but that would mean they would keep marching right up to the protected zone. It could place the tribe in danger.' Mirka said.

'How many do you think there are?' Granddad asked.

'At least fifty plus the two barclues.' Mirka answered.

'Well, if we can't hide, we have to fight.' Granddad replied.

Granddad looked around at the open space they found themselves in. He looked to the tree line on either side and then to the others. All the trees were bare or dead, but their sheer number would provide cover. He called them all to him and quickly ran over a plan.

*****

Graff marched at the front of his troops. This wasn't a sign of bravery although it could be mistaken for that. The two barclues were at the back, and Graff wanted as much distance as possible between them and him. Every now and then one of them would roar causing him to jump. He hoped none of his men noticed. He was starting to sweat as the ground began to rise. Graff knew they were getting close to the protected zone which also meant they might be close to Jacob.

He had thirty trolls, twenty-five goblins and the two barclues. Surely this would be enough to take care of Jacob and his men. Something was bothering Graff, though. He was sure the Master had wanted to kill Jacob herself, so why send him to do it for her. Maybe it was his reward for loyalty or for getting Jacob here. It sounded good in his head, but Graff doubted those were the reasons. Suddenly the reality of the situation hit him square in the chest. He was being sent to his death. The Master didn't think for one minute that he could defeat Jacob. He couldn't run away as that may anger a barclue. For the first time in his life, he would have to fight.

They reached the top of the slope and came out into a clearing that he had been in hundreds of times in the past. Something didn't feel right, though. The thick black hairs on his neck stood up. He looked around and could see no reason for this feeling. The other trolls and goblins clearly didn't notice anything and kept marching.

Soon they were all in the clearing and the feeling of unease in Graff grew. When the first bomb was thrown from inside the tree line, Graff wasn't sure what it was. At first, he thought it was a bird. Then he thought it was a rock. He watched, mesmerised, as the object flew through the air landing on the right side of the group. The instant flash and the screams of pain and anguish soon let him know what was happening. Goblins and trolls exploded sending pus, ooze and ash in every direction.

Graff was hit in the face by part of an exploded troll. Dizzied and panicked he ran back and forth with his short dagger drawn. He looked for the source of the bombs but could see nothing. The barclues were roaring and becoming more and more restless. Arrows came next. They flew in from both sides. The sound of them cutting through the wind was the sound of whistling death to several trolls at the rear of the group. Their numbers were reducing by the second, and still, Graff had not even seen the enemy.

The barclues broke ranks and began charging through the trolls and goblins looking for the hidden enemy. Just then, in front of them, Graff saw a small group emerge from the trees. It was the boys and the Vikings. One of the barclues saw them and roared before charging. Graff watched as the boy who had stopped the Shifter raised his left arm, and three objects flew out slamming into the barclue. The large creature stopped in its tracks and looked down at the wounds. Three holes had appeared across its chest and stomach. A look of confusion spread across its face as the barclue fell backwards and lay still.

Graff looked at the boy who was still holding his arm up and fear spread through him. He had to get away from this battle. He turned to run and tripped over a goblin standing behind him. Graff hit the ground hard and was just coming to his senses when he saw the second barclue charging towards the enemy. Unfortunately for Graff, he realised too late that he was in its path.

The barclue didn't break stride as it crushed Graff under its powerful legs. He lay still as his breathing began to slow. Graff wouldn't have to fight in this battle after all.

George watched the second barclue running towards him and didn't flinch. He fired off another three shots, this time hitting the head and body. They watched as the large beast collapsed instantly from the impact. The Vikings and Peter, raised their swords and led by Granddad, charged towards the enemy. The Elders broke out of their cover and continued to throw their bombs.

Mirka and the other tribespeople swooped down out of the trees and began picking off trolls and goblins with ease. The enemy didn't know which way to turn and before they could organise themselves into any kind of formation over half of them were dead.

Arto burst out of the trees, roaring as he ran at speed into the nearest trolls. Screams and howls of pain erupted as the large bear attacked. The Vikings began cutting down the goblins near them, and Peter took down one particularly large troll with a dodge and swipe of his sword.

He watched as three trolls cornered Zyanya against a large rock at the side of the clearing. He began to run towards her when something stopped him in his tracks. The trolls advanced, eager to kill one of their enemies. As they got closer, Zyanya vanished. The trolls were stunned and began looking around in confusion.

Before they could regain their senses, Zyanya appeared behind them and fired off two arrows killing one troll. The other two charged, but Zyanya vanished again, this time, reappearing on top of the rock and fired off three quick shots, killing the other two trolls.

Peter watched mesmerised as Zyanya took down the three trolls. She looked towards him and smiled. Her facial expression changed, and Peter turned to see a goblin running towards him. He heard the whistle of the arrow flying past his ear and watched as the goblin hit the ground. Peter turned to thank Zyanya, but she had vanished again. He shook his head and joined the Vikings in the attack against the trolls and goblins.

From this close, it was dangerous for the Elders to use their bombs and potions, so they stood behind the Vikings, Arto and the tribespeople and became spectators to the fight. The speed of the Vikings was matched only by Mirka and the others.

The goblins and trolls were cut down quickly. Any that tried to run soon ended up on the ground with an arrow in their back. Zyanya kept appearing and firing one or two arrows before disappearing again.

Within minutes the battle was over. The clearing was covered in the bodies of trolls and goblins. Peter couldn't stop staring at Zyanya. He still could not believe what he had seen her do. He had seen so many things in the past few days, but nothing prepared him for a girl that could vanish at will.

'I think we can assume the Master knows we are coming. She will have worked out that we were waiting for daylight to move through the forest.' Granddad said.

'This could be the first of many attacks on our journey, we need to stay alert.' Mirka added.

'I agree, I think we should keep moving. If anything else heard this battle we don't want to be here when it comes to investigate.' Granddad said looking wearily into the trees.

Peter looked at George and although neither of them said anything it was clear they were both thinking the same thing. *Granddad thinks the Shifter might be close.*

The group moved off quickly with Arto and Mirka at the front. Peter found himself walking next to Zyanya.

'How do you do that?' he asked her.

'Do what?' she replied without looking at him.

'How do you disappear?'

'I've always been able to do it. My father said I was born this way.' Zyanya finally looked at Peter as she spoke.

'They tell me it's my gift.' she added.

'What about those two? I never noticed them doing anything unusual during the fight.' Peter asked pointing at the tribespeople with Mirka.

'They are excellent trackers and the best shots in the tribe. The one on the right is Kale. He can hit any target he can see. The other is Bryal he always goes with the hunting parties to protect them from attack. They volunteered to come with you.'

'Why would they do that?' Peter asked.

'It's a chance to get close to the Master. To kill the witch who stole our world.' Zyanya replied.

'Is that why you're here?'

'No, I'm here because of him.' She replied pointing at Granddad.

'What do you mean?'

'I grew up listening to your Gran tell tales of the Viking warrior who saved the world from the Master. Now he's here maybe we can save our world too.'

The pair walked on in silence. Peter began to realise that his Granddad being here was a sign of hope not just for James and Charlotte but for this world as well.

The Shifter looked at the bodies of the trolls and goblins. He saw the two barclues almost side by side. The Shifter walked over to them and looked at their wounds. Whatever had been used was very effective. He would need to be careful. He walked back through the battle scene and stopped. He looked down at the body of Graff and smiled. Finally, someone had ended the life of the worthless troll. The Shifter left the clearing and began to follow the path taken by Jacob and the others. Soon they would find out how powerful an enemy he was.

Chapter 8

The Master held Charlotte's arm as she led her back towards the beam of light. Even the touch of her fingers made Charlotte feel uncomfortable. She tried not to squirm or flinch. Charlotte had no idea what the Master wanted with her and wasn't sure she wanted to find out.

'You don't have to fear me, Charlotte. I mean you no harm. I promise you that while you're by my side, no one will hurt you.' The Master spoke in a soothing voice Charlotte had never heard her use before.

'What do you mean? You kidnapped my brother and me. How can I believe that?'

'Taking you and James was required. I needed a reason to get Jacob here. Peter's friends were the easiest way.' The Master seemed almost apologetic when she spoke.

'What will you do with us?'

'Once Jacob has been defeated James can return home if that's what you want. He's of no use to me. You on the other hand are very important.' The Master looked at Charlotte as she spoke and tightened her grip on her arm.

Charlotte tried to fight the urge to struggle even though the grip on her arm was getting sore. They continued to walk and began climbing the walkway around the beam of light. Suddenly the Master let go of Charlotte. Charlotte rubbed her arm and looked at the mark the

Master's touch had left. A perfect red hand mark which showed every finger began to fade on her skin. Charlotte had her back to the light as she faced the Master.

'Why am I important to you?' she asked still rubbing her arm.

'I lost two sisters when Jacob attacked our ship. Years before I lost my only daughter. I'm alone here Charlotte. I have my armies, servants and slaves, but that's not enough. None of them could replace my family.'

'You can't mean that I'll replace them?' Charlotte asked.

'Would it be so bad? Staying here with me, and becoming as powerful as I am.' The Master took a step forward as she spoke. Charlotte tried to back away but couldn't as she was on the edge of the walkway.

'You're not serious?' Charlotte said in a bewildered voice.

'Trust me, Charlotte; I'm very serious.'

The Master took a step forward, and without another word pushed Charlotte backwards. Charlotte screamed and fell into the beam of light where she was suspended in the air unable to move. The Master began to chant in a rhythmic tone. The beam of light intensified in colour. The Master raised her arms and chanted louder. Charlotte was able to move her head slightly and looked down at the cauldron which was smoking intensely and changing colour rapidly.

A beam of dark green light began to emerge up the stream moving towards Charlotte. There was nothing she could do but watch it approaching. Finally, the dark green light reached her and began to move all around her. Charlotte felt it press against her skin as if it was looking for a way inside. The light felt heavy as it slowly worked its way up her legs and body. Charlotte screamed, and the light appeared to go into her mouth.

Suddenly Charlotte was quiet; she closed her mouth and eyes. The Master watched as Charlotte remained perfectly still for a few minutes and the green light began to fade. The Master took a step forward and motioned with her hand. Charlotte floated down out of the light and onto the walkway. Her body folded, and she fell onto the ground face down.

The Master turned Charlotte over and waited for her to open her eyes. She whispered her name as softly as a mother would do to a child who was having a nightmare. Charlotte began to flex her fingers and move her feet. She moved her head and finally opened her eyes.

Gone were the big greenish hazel eyes and in their place were eyes as black as coal surrounded by a faint yellow. The Master smiled when she saw those eyes. Charlotte sat up and looked around. She looked down at herself and stretched her arms out in front of her. She made fists with her hands then pointed her fingers up into the air. A blue light began to appear at her fingertips. Charlotte brought her arms back down to her side and looked at the Master and smiled.

'How do you feel?' the Master asked.

'Magnificent.' Charlotte replied.

'Come, we have much work to do.' The Master said ushering Charlotte back down the walkway.

'Lead on Master.' Charlotte replied. The Master smiled, and the pair disappeared into the darkness.

Chapter 9

The group continued through the forest always on the lookout for further enemies. They had travelled for another hour without seeing or hearing anything out of the ordinary. Peter could hear the river now as the forest began to thin out slightly and they continued towards the cave system. Black dust floated in the air like snow being blown by the wind.

George was walking next to Porr and Tofi and every now and then he was sure he heard someone, or something, whisper his name. It was so faint and seemed to be carried on a breeze that he was never sure if he had heard it or not. No one else reacted so he thought he must have been hearing things and continued to walk without mentioning it.

'George.'

The whisper came again, this time, over to his right, but again very faint. He looked at Porr and Tofi, but neither showed any sign that they had heard the voice. George shook his head, rubbed his forehead and continued.

The Shifter had caught up with the group and was matching them stride for stride. He moved unseen by his enemy, but this was not the time to attack. In the forest, he might lose his advantage, especially with the tribal Elders and the girl here.

He had seen her before; seen how she could disappear at will. He respected her gift and had learned a great deal about her. He wondered if she even knew the truth. She was dangerous; she had more power than she realised. As she grew, she would become stronger. There was no doubt about it she was a truly worthy adversary.

As for the boy, the one who had dared to mock him in the caves of the Cove, what was he without his weapon? Nothing more than a scared boy. The Shifter had no doubts it was the boy who had brought down the barclues. This pleased him as it meant the boy would be confident in his weapon's ability to stop even the Shifter. The foolishness of children always amused him. The Shifter became lost in his thoughts, had he ever been a child? He didn't remember if he had. He remembers his first battle and every battle since but nothing before this.

The Shifter watched the boy. He had decided it was time to have some fun, to start sowing seeds of doubt in his young head. He focussed fully on the boy; he let the others disappear from his sight. His thoughts became entirely about the boy. He watched as the boy became uncomfortable and began to scratch unconsciously at his forehead.

The Shifter smiled; the boy could feel his presence. The Shifter whispered his name. He watched as George looked around. He could see the confusion cross over his face. Had he heard his name? Was it the wind? The

Shifter liked this game. It would pass the time until he was ready to attack.

George was becoming more and more uneasy. He was sure he heard his name, and his head was starting to hurt. It was clear no one else was hearing anything. He hurried away from Porr and Tofi and caught up with Peter and his Granddad.

'Please don't think I'm mad, but I keep hearing someone whispering my name.' George said looking at both of them.

'When did you start hearing it?' Granddad replied not questioning George's sanity at all.

'It started about five minutes ago. It's the faintest whisper, but I'm sure I hear it.'

'When was the last time you heard it?'

'Just before I ran over to you. Neither Porr or Tofi heard it so I didn't want to say to them in case they thought I was scared or mad.'

'When you hear it again give me a nod and point to where you think it came from.' Granddad said.

George agreed, and the three walked silently onwards following the tribespeople and Arto. Suddenly George nodded and pointed to the right just in front of them. Granddad looked where George had pointed and thought he caught a glimmer of movement.

'Do the same the next time you hear it.' He said to George.

No sooner were the words out his mouth than George nodded and pointed to his left. Granddad looked round and again just the faintest glimmer before the forest returned to normal.

'Stay with Peter. I don't think you're mad George, and I don't think we're alone.'

Granddad signalled to Porr and Tofi to guard the boys before he left them and hurried up to Mirka, Arto and the tribespeople. The boys watched as he talked with them and pointed towards where George said he had last heard the voice coming from. Arto came back and stood in front of the boys while the tribespeople fanned out with their bows drawn.

'What is it Arto? What does Granddad think is out there?' Peter asked.

'He's not sure Peter, but he thinks he saw something.' Arto replied never taking his eyes off the place where George had last heard the voice.

Peter drew his sword and waited nervously for an attack, but no attack came. The Elders came close to Arto and surveyed the forest. They all watched the charred lifeless trees, but there was nothing to see. They stood motionless listening to the forest, but the voice didn't come again. Granddad looked at George and asked a silent question with his expression. George shook his head in response. Granddad nodded, signalled to Mirka, and slowly they began to move.

The Shifter was enjoying this. He couldn't help but be impressed with Jacob. He wasn't sure how, but he was certain Jacob had seen him. Just to be sure he moved to the other side and said the boy's name again. Jacob looked right at him. The Shifter stared back before vanishing further into the dead trees. He shifted shape again and took to the skies.

He watched as they spread out and hunted for whatever it was in the forest. It wouldn't be that easy. Did they expect him to come charging out and attack them? He had learned that a direct attack against this enemy was not the best move.

They began to move off again obviously satisfied that the threat had gone. The Shifter couldn't resist one last bit of fun. 'I'm coming for you George, soon oh very soon.'

George heard the voice as clear as day.

'I heard it again, from above us!' he shouted.

All the arrows pointed to the sky, but there was nothing there.

'What did it say?' Arto asked.

'It said, it said it's coming for me. That's all it said. It's coming for me soon.' George sounded scared. His voice made him sound like the child he was.

'We have to keep moving. Whatever it is doesn't want to attack us now. If it did, it would have already. Keep moving everyone.' Granddad motioned for them all to keep moving as he talked.

Mirka moved to Granddad and spoke quietly.

'Do you think it was the Shifter?' he asked.

'Who else would it be? George is the one who defeated him in the Cove. We must protect him.' Granddad replied.

'I'm going to send Kale and Bryal ahead to scout the ground and make sure there are no surprises for us.'

Granddad nodded and Mirka shouted the two men over. He told them what he wanted and without another word they ran off ahead of the group.

'I should go. I can move faster than either of them and can evade any enemy.' Zyanya said.

'That's exactly why we need you to stay with us. If we are attacked again, we will need your skill, Zyanya.' Mirka replied.

Zyanya didn't argue the point any further and moved to the front of the group with her bow ready. The dead forest would soon be behind them, and the caves could be much more dangerous.

Chapter 10

'Come with me; there's something I want to explain to you.' The Master said to Charlotte, who nodded her head in response and followed on.

As they walked, they came across two trolls. One saw Charlotte walking quietly behind the Master and decided that Charlotte was intending to sneak up on her.

'Behind you Master.' Te shouted and started to run towards Charlotte with his crude sword drawn.

The Master smiled and stepped aside to watch this troll try bravely to save her. Not for one second did she consider telling him the truth, that Charlotte was now with them. The troll raised his sword and was about strike when Charlotte raised both her hands and two blue bolts of lightning shot out. The troll was thrown backwards and landed heavily on the ground, his sword clattering next to him.

The other troll, confused by what he had seen, looked to the Master and then to Charlotte. If he was waiting for some sign from the Master, he was waiting in vain. The Master was enjoying this little show. What would the troll do? Would he realise that Charlotte was with them and not attack or would he try to defend his Master? Poor stupid troll the Master thought as it charged Charlotte shouting something about defending the Master till his death, which was going to be very soon.

Charlotte saw the second troll coming and viewed it about as threatening as a ladybug would be to a snake. She opened her arms wide and floated into the air. The troll dived at the space Charlotte had moved from and landed flat on his face in the dirt. Scrambling back to his feet he grunted, grabbed his sword, and stood between the Master and Charlotte.

'I'll protect you, Master. Stay behind me and this girl will not harm you.' The troll said in his gruff spluttering voice.

'You are very brave.' The Master replied.

Charlotte looked at the Master and smiled. The Master smiled back, and Charlotte floated down to the ground and made one motion with her left hand which made the troll drop his sword. She flicked her right hand dismissively at him, and he was thrown hard into a large rock. The troll lay motionless.

Charlotte raised her arms and both trolls lifted off the ground, their bodies limp and broken from the brief fight. She held them there effortlessly looking at each troll in turn. The Master put her hand on Charlotte's shoulder.

'That's enough fun now Charlotte.' The Master said.

'Why did they attack?' Charlotte asked letting both trolls drop to the ground.

'They thought you were going to harm me.' The Master replied.

'Why would I harm you?'

'You wouldn't Charlotte, but trolls are very protective of me.'

'You need better protection.' Charlotte replied looking back at the bodies.

'I have Tolldruck and the Shifter, and now I have you.' The Master said smiling at Charlotte before continuing.

'Enough of this sideshow, there's something I want to show you.'

They walked to where the large cauldron shot up its dazzling light.

'What does it do?' Charlotte asked.

'This cauldron allows us to live on the surface as we do underground. The beam of light is gradually changing the atmosphere to suit us. Without it, we would be weaker and easier to kill. If the change happens too fast, we will destroy the planet,' the Master replied.

Charlotte watched as the Master placed her hand in the beam of light and seemed to go into a trance. She stayed like that for a few minutes before removing her hand and turning to Charlotte.

'You know we used to go to your world, and always had to hurry there and back within three days. It wasn't easy getting there and stealing enough children, sheep or eggs in that short amount of time, but that was all the time we could spend away from this place. Any longer and we would die. Then something marvellous happened.' The Master paused.

'What happened?' Charlotte asked.

'Men began to advance; they began to create and build increasingly. With more building came more machines and factories. This caused more pollution, and your atmosphere gradually became suitable for us. We were able to stay for longer without any effect on our bodies. Then finally the Earth became so polluted that we could live there and walk amongst you. We're not as strong there as we are here, not yet.'

'So, man is turning the world into a second home for you?'

'Yes Charlotte, and once we have full control of this world, both above and below ground, we will look to your world next.'

'Why do you need children?'

'There is something else I must show you which will answer your question.'

Without another word, the Master moved to the wall behind the cauldron and raised her hands. She whispered softly, and the wall began to move. Within a few seconds, a doorway had been created, and light could be seen coming from the other side.

The Master walked through and signalled Charlotte to follow. Charlotte walked behind the Master and found herself in a large room in which the ceiling glowed faintly. At the far side, there was a rough stone staircase leading down. The pair walked to the staircase and started down. Instead of getting darker as they got further underground it actually began to get lighter. A strange glowing light that changed from blue to green to purple illuminated the staircase.

They came to the end of the stairs, and Charlotte gasped. In front of her was a huge gemstone seemingly suspended over a lava-filled hole. Steam rose up from the bubbling lava, and the stone appeared orange on the underside because of it. The stone changed colour over and over casting the strange light all over the room.

Once her eyes had adjusted to the strange glow, Charlotte looked at the top of the gemstone and could see five vines running from it into the roof of the cave.

'Do they go to the cauldron?' she asked.

'Yes, they do.' The Master replied.

'What's this gemstone for?' Charlotte asked.

'This holds the true-life force of my kind. It comes from deep within this world's core. It's also a prison.'

'What do you mean?' Charlotte asked moving closer as she did.

'Look closely at the stone Charlotte.' The Master replied.

Charlotte got as close as she dared to the lava pit and stared into the gemstone. She could make out something in the centre. As her eyes adjusted, she began to make out a shape.

'Is that a person in there?' she asked doubtfully.

'Yes, it is Charlotte. That's the body of the first witch Master. She was the most powerful witch ever to have lived. Her magic brought trolls, goblins and other creatures into this world.'

'If she's so powerful, how did she end up in there?'

'I put her there.' The Master replied without a hint of remorse.

'Why would you do that?'

'She lacked vision, Charlotte. She didn't want to conquer worlds. She was happy living underground only coming up to steal children when it was required. She invented trolls and goblins to help us create great cave systems we could live in. She didn't like being above the ground. Finally, after she refused to see the benefits from living like the rulers we were meant to be I could no longer follow her.'

'Why didn't she want to be above the ground?'

'She gave me many reasons none of which I accepted. She said we would risk the death of our kind. Risk becoming too exposed to the world above us. I waited for my chance and together with my sisters we overthrew her and imprisoned her inside the gemstone.'

'You still haven't told me why you need to steal children?'

'Children's fear helps with our magic. We use their tears and sweat in some of our most powerful potions. Or we drink it to increase our magic. They are also good slaves who can work in small spaces to help dig our caves.'

'Where do you keep them?'

'We have an extensive prison system deeper underground. There are not too many children there just now. Jacob has stopped us bringing them back from your world and those that are left here are in the protected forests.'

'Why did you have to move above ground?' Charlotte asked still staring at the gemstone.

'Why should we live underground when there is so much to conquer above it?' the Master replied. She took a couple of steps towards the gemstone before continuing.

'We had done all we could do below the surface. A race as powerful as ours belongs above the ground. We shouldn't be hiding from men when we could easily rule them. Men grew confident in their abilities and believed themselves to be top of the food chain. I changed that. It's a shame the first Witch Master had to be overthrown. She just didn't see my vision for what it was.'

'Now you are the Master, and we all follow you.' Charlotte smiled as she spoke.

'You will be by my side for centuries Charlotte. Together we will conquer the forests then your world. The one world I want is proving more difficult to achieve than all the others.'

'Which world is that?'

'The dragon world, it's perfect for us. We've tried before but were defeated. Our army was almost completely wiped out. I've been creating another one, though. Down below us in the deepest caves of this underworld, they are waiting to be woken up.' The Master smiled as she spoke and looked into the distance.

'How do we travel between worlds? How do the portals work?' Charlotte asked.

'You're eager to learn; I like that. Come with me and I'll show you.' The Master said no more, turned and walked away.

Charlotte looked confused as the Master didn't walk back towards the stairs. She walked towards the far wall and as she approached a portal appeared. Charlotte watched as the Master stepped through the portal and vanished.

Charlotte approached the place where the Master had disappeared with some caution. She took slow, steady steps, and as she got closer, the portal began to appear. Faintly at first, but as she continued to walk the portal began to glow brightly. Charlotte breathed hard as she walked through. There was a flash of light and sensation of heat, and then she was standing in the middle of a room with the Master by her side.

'Where are we?' Charlotte asked.

'We're deeper underground now. This is where we create the portals.'

'How do you create them?'

'They are created by the Mystics,' the Master replied.

As soon as she said it, three figures appeared in the room. They were ghostly white with featureless faces, and all wearing red cloaks. They seemed to float rather than walk as they came closer.

'Show her the portals.' The Master ordered.

The Mystics turned and floated away silently. The Master and Charlotte followed them into another room.

The Mystics stood in the centre and raised their arms. Above them, several shapes began to form. Slowly the shapes changed into glowing spheres. The spheres took on shapes and soon Charlotte understood what she was looking at.

'That's my planet, that's the Earth,' she said approaching one of them.

'You're right Charlotte, and this is Zanthura where you are now. The tribes have another name for it, Vultraha.' The Master said pointing to one of the other globes.

One of the Mystics motioned with their hands and the Earth globe moved forward and spun quickly until the sea near Campbell's Cove was visible. The other Mystic did the same with the globe of Zanthura. It spun until the sea where they had come through the portal was showing. The two Mystics reached into their cloaks and took out small red orbs. They dropped the orbs into the globes, and they flashed brightly before falling into the sea in each world. Instantly the portals glowed then disappeared.

'How do they do that?' Charlotte asked.

'Mystics are not like us. They don't have physical bodies like we do. They live in a shadow world that allows them to create links between universes and solar systems. They are not restricted by the laws of physics or even the laws of magic.'

'If they are so powerful, how do you get them to serve you?' Charlotte asked.

'They don't serve me. Mystics serve no one. The first Witch Master refused to talk to the Mystics; she said they were dangerous. I took over and now we have an arrangement with them. Mystics feed on the souls of living things. We provide those souls.' The Master smiled before continuing. 'In return, they build us our portals to other worlds. It's ingenious. They take a fragment of the gemstones that link all of my kind and infuse them with their magic. This means that only when one of us approaches will the portal open.'

'Why Campbell's Cove? Why do the portals open there?' Charlotte peered at the worlds floating in the arms of the Mystics.

'Many years ago, we found the Cove. The cave systems there are fantastic. Do you know how many minerals and rare metals are buried deep in those caves? It's an amazing place, and it's quiet which allowed us to build a base without ever being disturbed. The original plan was to stay there and steal children, and mine the minerals and metals.'

'What changed?' Charlotte asked.

'A few things. Goblins and trolls are stupid and can go exploring for food. Shadow walkers are also known for their tendency to drift away on their own adventures. People became suspicious, and we had to create other portals that would allow dragons to cross into your world. The hope was that this would make humans believe the dragons were to blame for their children and livestock going missing.' The Master paused and looked at the spinning globes. She shook her head and continued.

'Then Jacob came, and they found the imprisoned dragon. That changed everything. We were unable to continue with our plan. We had to be patient. We returned when we assumed that Jacob would be long dead. We were wrong.'

'Couldn't you just move the portal to somewhere else?'

'The minerals and metals there are unique to your world. It took us years to find the Cove, and it is perfect for our needs. We need to defeat Jacob, and we need to kill off what remains of the tribes. Once we have done that we can return to the cove and begin to build our army there. In those caves in Campbell's Cove, I could build an army stronger than any you could imagine.'

'What kind of army? How do you plan to defeat the tribes if you can't reach them?' Charlotte asked.

'We have much to discuss, and I have more to show you. Come with me and I will answer both of those questions. Together we are going to wipe out all our enemies.'

Chapter 11

Kale and Bryal moved through the forest at pace. They got close to the treeline by the water and followed it towards the caves. Moving silently, and with confidence, they knew how important this was; they had been entrusted by Mirka to make sure the way forward for the others was safe.

So far nothing had crossed their path, and nothing seemed unusual or out of place. Neither of them had their weapons drawn as they could move quicker without them.

Kale turned to Bryal and pointed into the distance and nodded. They were close to the caves now and running side by side. Kale turned back to face the way they were moving and was caught in a vice like grip. Bryal suddenly aware of the danger moved in to help his friend with incredible speed. He wasn't fast enough though as another arm grabbed him by the neck and lifted him off the ground.

Both tribesmen struggled and fought, but neither could free themselves from Tolldruck's grip.

'You're in a hurry. You almost took me by surprise.' Tolldruck said moving his stare over both of them.

He held them off the ground effortlessly, tightening his grip slightly causing both men great pain.

'Where are you going in such a rush?' Tolldruck asked.

Bravely neither man replied. Tolldruck squeezed harder almost crushing their necks.

'Where are the others? I know you're not out here alone.'

Bryal looked at Tolldruck and signalled that he wanted to speak. Tolldruck loosened his grip enough to let him.

'We're scouting,' Bryal said.

'You're scouting? Is that the best you can do?' Tolldruck replied.

'We were sent out to look for the enemy before the others left. To make sure it's safe.' Bryal replied. His voice had a raw rasping sound to it.

'Tell me, did you encounter a small force of goblins and trolls on this scouting trip?' Tolldruck asked.

The two men looked at each other for a split second, but it was long enough for Tolldruck to know Bryal was lying. Without another thought, he snapped his neck and threw him to the ground.

'Let's try again.' He said to Kale.

'What are you doing out here without the others?' he continued.

'Making sure the path is clear.' Kale said.

'Did you see the trolls?' Tolldruck asked.

Kale nodded his head in response.

'Where are they now?' Tolldruck asked, relaxing his grip some more to allow Kale to answer.

'They're all dead.' Kale smiled as he spoke.

'All of them? Are you sure?' Tolldruck asked.

Again, Kale nodded his head wearily and smiled defiantly.

'If they're all dead, why do you need to check the path?' Tolldruck asked.

'Something else here.' Kale's voice had begun to sound distant as the constant pressure on his neck took effect.

'What was it?' Tolldruck asked.

'We never saw it, but it was there.'

Tolldruck stared into Kale's face, smiled then crushed the life out of him in an instant. He dropped the lifeless body to the ground. It would seem that Graff had been died unless the coward had managed to avoid the fight once again. Tolldruck was interested in the other thing the scout had said, 'something else here' could he have meant the Shifter? Was the Shifter waiting for them in the caves? Tolldruck looked around for signs the Shifter had come this way but saw nothing.

If they had decided to send two men on ahead it meant they felt the threat was very real. Tolldruck decided to head for the caves. He looked at the bodies of the men and left them where they lay, a present for Jacob and his Vikings.

*****

Arto strode forward at the front of the group with Mirka and Granddad. The others followed close behind. It was clear to Granddad that the Elders were becoming nervous. They dropped back further, and every sound seemed to make them jump.

'Do your Elders come out of the protected zone often?' he asked Mirka.

'No, hardly ever. They make up the potions and weapons but leave the dangerous part to my men and me. I was surprised they wanted to come with us.'

'They seem nervous.'

'I noticed that as well, this is probably the furthest they've ever been.' Mirka replied glancing back at the Elders.

Arto stopped suddenly bringing the conversation to an end. He stood alertly sniffing the air. Porr and Tofi moved in closer to Peter and George with their swords drawn.

'What is it Arto?' Granddad asked.

'A familiar smell, there's something evil close by.' The bear replied.

They walked silently finding the path near the river and followed its course towards the caves. Arto was the first to see them. He gave out a low roar and ran ahead of the others who struggled to keep up. They burst out onto the path and saw the bodies lying near each other. Porr, Tofi and Mirka drew their weapons and watched the forest as the Elders moved in to check on Kale and Bryal. It was obvious that both were dead, and no amount of potions would bring them back. Elder Thomson looked at Granddad and shook his head.

'It doesn't make sense.' Arto said to no one in particular.

'What doesn't?' Peter asked.

'Why kill them and leave them where we would find them.'

'To make us frightened.' Granddad said. He looked at the others before continuing. 'Whatever is in this forest knows we are here and had no trouble killing two very good men. This is no troll or goblin that's stalking us.'

He could see the fear in Baden and Jeron's faces. Granddad looked at Mirka who nodded to confirm he could see it too.

'Baden and Jeron, I would like you to go back to the village and make sure we have enough potions and weapons in case there is an attack. Alert, all the soldiers, to be ready just in case.' Mirka said.

The Elders looked at each other and could barely hide their delight at being sent back.

'We can't afford to send anyone with you, though. You need to move quickly and quietly. Whatever this thing is that's playing with us would appear to be in front of us. I don't think you'll come across any enemies, but you must be on your guard.'

Mirka looked at each Elder as he spoke.

'We will go and protect our home.' Baden said. Without another word, they turned and ran. Within a minute or so they were gone from sight.

'Why did you do that? There are so few of us.' George looked to Mirka and Granddad for an explanation.

'They were terrified; I could see it at the battle with the trolls and goblins. It was more evident after what happened with you in the forest. Seeing two men, two of their friends, killed seemingly without being able to put up a struggle was the final straw.' Mirka replied.

'Mirka's right George. They would have needed protecting if we had met any other enemies. We are better off with a smaller stronger group.' Granddad added.

'We're only ten now. What about our Elders? Are their lives not worth as much as Baden and Jeron?' Peter asked.

'Peter, Elders Thomson and Sanderson have been in many fights before. They have helped us countless times in the past and are vital to us succeeding.' Granddad looked from Peter to the two Elders as he spoke.

The Elders looked at Peter and nodded their heads.

'We will bury them here before we go any further. We can't leave them on the path like this. We'll give them a proper burial when we return.' Mirka was already moving to the scorched earth of the forest.

He used his bow as a makeshift shovel and then fell onto his hands and knees to continue digging. One by one the others joined in. Arto used his powerful front legs to dig the second grave.

Very quickly Bryal and Kale were buried in the burnt earth beneath a huge tree. Mirka marked the charred trunk with his dagger. He knelt before each grave and closed his eyes. He picked up a handful of earth each time and threw it on the graves.

'Their deaths will not be for nothing. We will find your friends and we will kill the Master.' Mirka said directly to Granddad.

Granddad nodded his head in response and turned to begin the journey once more.

'How much farther to the caves?' Arto asked Mirka.

'Not long, we will be there soon.' Mirka replied.

Peter looked at Zyanya and could see she had tears running down her face. He walked over to her, unsure what he was going to say or do.

'Zyanya, I'm sorry that your people died.' It sounded blunt when the words came out, and Peter instantly wished he could have taken them back.

Zyanya stared at Peter. The tear tracks were clear on her face.

'I should have gone with them. I could have stopped this from happening.' She said.

'You might have ended up lying next to them.' It was all he could think to say, and again as soon as the words were out, he wished he could take them back.

'With my gift, my ability, I could have saved them. Mirka should have let me go with them. He wanted me to stay to protect you and your friends. What makes your life more valuable than theirs?' She asked, pointing at the two graves.

'I don't think he expected them to die or come into danger. They were your best trackers and great scouts, weren't they?' Peter asked.

'Yes, they were.'

'Then whatever did that to them was powerful and fast. If they didn't see it, then maybe you wouldn't have either.' Peter knew he sounded harsh, but he didn't mean to.

Zyanya looked at him with sad eyes.

'I would have liked the chance to try and save them.' She said before turning and walking away.

Peter went to follow her, but Elder Thomson put his hand on his shoulder.

'Let her go, Peter. She needs time to come to terms with this. Anything you say now may cause an argument. You mean well, and you're right, she knows that, but she needs time to let it sink in.'

'I sounded so harsh, so uncaring.'

'Give her some time Peter.' Elder Thomson smiled at Peter and squeezed his shoulder.

'We need to go now; the others are getting ahead of us.' Elder Thomson pointed to the path where George and the others were now about five hundred metres ahead of them.

Peter and Elder Thomson rushed to catch up. As they came alongside Zyanya, she looked at them and then vanished into thin air. A couple of seconds later she reappeared closer to the main group. Peter looked at Elder Thomson.

'She'll come round Peter, she's hurt and blames us in a way for her friends' deaths.'

'No, I don't think so. I think she blames herself.' Peter replied.

At the front, Granddad was talking to Mirka about the caves and what lay beyond.

'How many times have you been into this cave system?' Granddad asked.

'I've been in it countless times. As children, some of our scouting lessons took place near the river and in the caves.' Mirka replied.

'Are they well lit?'

'Some parts are lit with fire fungus although there are very dark patches especially deep into the system. It will take some time to get through the caves even if we don't meet any enemies.'

'When was the last time you were in the caves?'

'Not long ago. We had received information from one of our scouts that the area appeared to have been abandoned by the enemy. Several scouting trips over several weeks had shown the area to be quiet. There was no one there. No trolls, goblins or barclues. This was very unusual as the area was permanently guarded.' Mirka replied.

'Why did they leave?' Granddad asked.

'We don't know. We can only guess that either there's nothing there of any value to them or they don't ever think we would go in there.' Mirka replied. He looked at Granddad who had a worried look on his face.

'What is it?' Mirka asked.

'How far into the caves did you go after you knew this?' Granddad asked his question in response.

'Not far, we went into the first main chamber. It was clear there was nothing there. We have kept a watch on it ever since, but nothing has come in or out of this side of the caves.'

'Trolls and goblins are stupid, but the Master isn't. What if they don't go down there anymore because she's told them not to?'

'Why would she do that?' Mirka asked.

'Maybe there's something else down there.' Granddad replied.

The two men walked in silence both lost in their thoughts.

Chapter 12

Tolldruck approached the cave system with some caution. He had no idea where the Shifter was hiding, but he knew he didn't trust him. The Master had been wrong to bring the Shifter into this, and she knew it. Tolldruck would never say it to her, but they both knew. The Shifter had played his part in Campbell's Cove, but Tolldruck truly wished he had been killed by the boy.

Tolldruck could see the mouth of the caves near the riverbank. Everything looked peaceful and still. The path sloped down towards the caves as the river rose up above him. Tolldruck didn't know fear, but he was not stupid. He was alert for any sign of the Shifter.

Suddenly the wind began to blow, and dead leaves and bits of charred bark were picked up from the path and began to swirl round and round in front of Tolldruck. Slowly more leaves, dirt and bark began to join the mini hurricane.

'Enough with the dramatic entrance Shifter. The Master wants to see you.' Tolldruck spoke to the hurricane as if it was something he saw every day.

The hurricane stopped swirling, and the Shifter formed in front of Tolldruck.

'Why should I go to her? The boy is coming this way. I can kill them all and make him suffer for what he did to me.' The Shifter asked stepping forward and reducing the distance between the two.

'The Master has a plan, she doesn't need you making a mess of things.' Tolldruck responded taking a step closer as well. He was not afraid of the Shifter.

'She might be your Master, but she's not mine. Her plan didn't seem to be going so well last time I looked.' The Shifter snarled.

'She is the Master of all of us.'

'Do you really think that? You with all your strength, and talent for killing? Do you need a Master?'

'She has guided us well so far. We will defeat the Viking and his friends then nothing will stop us taking control of their world. She has something special planned for our enemies.'

'The Viking does not interest me now. I only want the boy. I will kill the boy and let the others go on. Will that satisfy your Master? If they go into those caves, we both know they might never reach the Master.' The Shifter smiled as he spoke.

'You will not attack them here Shifter. Let them get to the city and I promise you that you can do whatever you like to the boy and any of the others, but Jacob must be left to the Master.'

The Shifter stared at Tolldruck and smiled taking a step backwards.

'Can you promise me the boy will be mine?'

'I can. The Master wants Jacob; the fate of the others is not her concern.' Tolldruck answered.

'If you break that promise you and the Master will regret it.' The Shifter stared at Tolldruck unblinkingly as he spoke.

Tolldruck flashed out an arm and grabbed the Shifter by the throat. He lifted the Shifter off the ground and backed him up against the charred trunk of a large tree. The trunk snapped and cracked with the force of the impact.

'Never threaten me and never threaten the Master. I could snap your neck like the trunk of this tree.' Tolldruck growled as he spoke.

The Shifter smiled and changed shape with such blurring speed that Tolldruck soon found himself gripping only air as he stumbled against the tree, snapping the trunk further. Tolldruck turned in time to take the full force of the Shifter's right arm in his chest. The tree trunk exploded as Tolldruck crashed through it.

'It's not a threat. If you break your promise I will kill you.' The Shifter snarled and with that he was gone.

Tolldruck stumbled out of the tree and roared. The Shifter was becoming more unruly and, worryingly, he was getting stronger. He heard noises close by and ran up to the river and dived in. This was not the time to fight Jacob and the others.

*****

The roar shook the path and caused the dead trees to rattle. The group stopped and looked around them. Arto stood at the front with his nose raised to the air. Granddad, with his sword drawn, stood by his side. Cautiously they walked forward ready to defend themselves from any attack. Peter came alongside his Granddad. He held his shield close to his chest and his sword out by his side.

'What do you think it was?' Peter asked.

'Whatever it was, it was big and sounded angry.' Arto replied never taking his eyes off the path in front of them.

Mirka and Zyanya skirted in and out the treeline. They made no sound as they moved checking the edges of the dead forest for enemies. Mirka returned and shook his head; they had not found anything.

As the caves finally came into view, Arto stopped and sniffed the air. He lowered his head and sniffed the ground before walking over to the remains of a dead tree trunk.

'Something happened here.' The large bear said.

Mirka came over and looked at the marks on the ground. He walked to the tree trunk then went behind it and looked into the forest.

'Arto's right; something did happen here. Look at the footprints in the earth.' He said pointing at two distinct sets of prints.

'Something was thrown into that tree to destroy it like that. Something large.' He continued.

'Whatever it was seems to have left now. There are more things in these woods than us today.'

'Do you think it'll be safe to go through the caves?' Elder Thomson asked.

'Do you mean any safer than in a forest full of trolls, goblins and barclues? Not to mention whatever caused this.' Zyanya replied.

Elder Thomson looked at Zyanya but couldn't think of a response. He looked away first and kicked at the path lifting dirt and dead tree bark into the air.

'Zyanya's right. Staying out here could be just as dangerous as going into the caves. At least going in there gets us closer to Charlotte and James.' Granddad said.

'What are we waiting for? Our friends are counting on us.' Peter said as he walked towards the caves.

Arto looked at Granddad and nodded his head.

'He has your bravery Jacob.' The large bear said.

'You used to call it foolishness if I remember correctly.' Granddad replied.

'Sometimes there's not much difference between the two.' Arto said as they entered the mouth of the caves.

Tolldruck watched from the water as the group entered the cave. The Shifter didn't say that the girl was with them. This could change things. The Master would want to know that she is coming.

The girl is dangerous, maybe as dangerous as the Shifter. Tolldruck watched as the girl walked into the caves at the back of the group. He waited until they were out of sight before going under the water again and back to the Master.

Chapter 13

The caves were huge and made the caves of Campbell's Cove seem tiny in comparison. The mouth of the cave sloped down into a massive cavern that was lit here and there by fire fungus. The roof of the cave was very flat and smooth. The group travelled down the path onto the cavern floor. They looked around in awe. Even Arto seemed impressed.

'It's like an underground warehouse.' George said to Peter.

'It's the biggest cave I've ever seen.' Peter replied.

Granddad turned to Mirka and pointed at the roof then to the floor.

'Why is it so smooth? There are no stalactites coming down from the roof or stalagmites growing up.' He asked.

'Stala what and stala who?' George whispered to Peter.

'They are rocks that grow down or up. If you look at the caves there are none anywhere.' Peter whispered back while he waited to hear Mirka's response.

'There used to be. There were rock formations in several places, and large stalactites grew down all over the caves. I don't understand it.' Mirka replied looking around with a confused look on his face.

Elders Thomson and Sanderson moved closer to Porr and Tofi.

'I don't like that at all. How can the caves change so dramatically?' Elder Thomson asked.

'I've no idea, but I don't like it either. Caves shouldn't change like that unless there has been an earthquake or some other massive event.' Elder Sanderson replied.

Zyanya had remained quiet and now stood next to Arto with her bow drawn and ready to fire.

'What is it, Zyanya?' Mirka asked.

'I don't know, but something isn't right in these caves.' She replied.

'The girl's right. There's something in here.' Arto replied.

'Let's keep moving but keep on the lookout.' Mirka said before starting to walk.

The group closed in with the Elders and the boys near the middle. Tofi and Porr walked on either side with their swords drawn. Peter watched as Zyanya walked confidently at the front with Arto, Mirka and Granddad.

Peter nudged George then walked round Tofi and moved up next to his Granddad.

'It might be safer for you if you stay behind us Peter.' Granddad said.

'If I'm the next Viking warrior I should be walking at the front with you.' Peter replied.

'The boy is brave Jacob.' Mirka said looking at Peter.

'So am I.' said George as he stood next to Tofi protecting the Elders.

'It seems we are the only ones who require help.' Elder Sanderson said to Elder Thomson.

'I'm quite happy to stand behind everyone else.' Elder Thomson replied.

They continued to walk through the cavernous passages surrounded by an eerie silence. It wasn't like the caves of Campbell's Cove with rock pools and sounds of water and small unseen animals. In these caves there was nothing. No sound, no wind or water and the only thing that seemed to be alive was them.

Peter was growing in confidence with every step. He could see them getting to the city unchallenged and undiscovered. He worried about James and Charlotte and hoped they were ok. He knew they must be terrified and confused, but hoped they realised that he was coming to save them.

The caves sloped down deeper, and there was more fire fungus in this part. The fungus lit up the walls and roof of the cave. Even this far in the caves still had a strange smoothness. No rocks were sticking out, and nothing was hanging from the ceiling. Peter was deep in his own thoughts and didn't notice the others stop.

'Peter wait. Look up ahead.' Granddad said.

Peter came out of his thoughts and looked to the others. They had all stopped and were staring directly ahead. Peter noticed Zyanya and Mirka had drawn their weapons and were standing ready to fight. He turned and looked further up the cave. Peter wasn't sure what he was looking at.

'What is it?' he asked.

'It's the rocks.' Mirka replied.

'What do you mean it's the rocks?' Peter looked at Mirka as he spoke.

'It's the rocks that are missing from the caves.' Mirka said, never lowering his bow.

'Why are you pointing your arrows at them?'

'Something had to put them there Peter and whatever did it is very strong.'

Peter looked back to the rocks. They were piled high and wide in the centre of the caves. He could see rows of sharp pointed rocks and next to them rocks of all shapes and sizes.

The group approached slowly. Arto led the way, never taking his eyes off the rocks. George walked next to

Peter with the sunshine shooter ready to fire. Peter held his sword by his side with his shield in front of him. Neither of them had any clue what they were readying their weapons for. The Elders each held a sunshine bomb. Peter looked to his Granddad who had his sword ready and was looking straight ahead.

They got closer and closer to the rocks, and still, nothing moved. There was an eerie silence, and the atmosphere had become heavy. Something wasn't right, but no enemy had shown itself to them.

A low rumbling began; it was coming from all around them. It started off quietly then grew and grew. The group stopped and waited. Small stones started rolling across the cave floor towards the large pile of rocks.

Granddad held his sword ready, and Peter did the same. The group looked around them as the noise increased. The rumbling became deafening, rebounding off the cave. The Elders covered their ears, and Arto roared in pain as the noise level grew. Peter could feel his sword vibrating in his hand and didn't know how much longer he could hold on. Then as quickly as the noise came, it stopped.

The silence was so sudden and unexpected it was almost as unsettling as the noise. The group looked at each other with confused expressions. The only one who didn't was Arto who kept his eyes firmly on the large pile of rocks.

'What do you see Arto?' Granddad asked.

Before the bear could answer the rock pile moved. George looked on, open-mouthed, as the rocks shifted again. Slowly the rocks began to take on a shape as if something was controlling them. It was difficult, at first, to see what was forming. The group instinctively started to back away. Even Arto retreated a couple of steps.

The rocks continued to move and join together. Piece by piece a huge monster began to form. The beast towered above them, standing at least thirty feet tall. Made completely of rock the monster appeared to be watching them from its eyeless face. The only feature on the face was a huge mouth filled with razor sharp rocks as teeth. The body was massive, and on each shoulder were some of the larger spiked rocks. Powerful arms ended in clawed hands each containing four of the sharp, deadly looking rocks. Dust and small rocks tumbled off the monster as it finished forming. The beast somehow roared and stamped its feet, which caused the cave to shake, and small cracks appeared on the cave floor.

The monster charged without hesitation. Zyanya and Mirka fired arrows that bounced harmlessly off the beast making no impact. It swooped one powerful arm towards Zyanya who vanished just in time to dodge the deadly blow. The monster roared and turned its attention towards Peter and Granddad, who were standing together with their swords drawn.

'Stay focused Peter and move as it attacks. Bring your sword down on any part of it you can!' Granddad shouted.

The beast charged and Peter and Granddad rolled out of the way, both bringing their swords across the back of its legs. Sparks flew as metal met rock, but no damage was caused.

The rock monster turned and faced the Elders and George. As it charged, Elder Sanderson threw a liquid sunshine bomb that hit its target. The explosion was fierce, but the monster kept coming. George fired off four of the fire fungus arrow heads which shattered on impact and started to light up the monster. Again, there was no effect as the beast continued to charge. George screamed and lifted his left hand, firing off liquid nitrogen which stopped the beast in its tracks. The legs froze into position, and it appeared to look down on itself.

The Elders and George ran round to join Peter and Granddad as the monster continued to examine its legs. It roared loudly and broke free of the liquid nitrogen although this time there were cracks in the rock running down the legs. Mirka and Zyanya joined them as did Porr and Tofi. Arto stayed away from the rest of the group and roared loudly getting the monster's attention. It turned to face him and charged. Arto remained motionless next to the cave wall as the monster raced towards him. At the last second, Arto dived to the right and the rock monster, unable to stop, smashed into the cave wall and crumpled to the ground.

Instantly a large crack appeared and began to grow up the wall. Arto joined the others, and they watched the monster. Slowly it began to move and got back to its feet. It had lost half an arm in the impact, and part of its head was missing. Some of the razor-sharp teeth had been driven into its skull and were now sticking out all over.

Mirka reached into his backpack and took out a silver-coloured rope.

'Zyanya, can you distract the monster? Give me time to get near enough to use this?' Mirka asked signalling to the rope.

Zyanya looked to the rope and then to the rock monster which was regaining its senses. She smiled and nodded her head.

'How can she smile at being bait?' George asked to no one in particular.

Zyanya moved away from the group and fired off a couple of arrows. They had no effect on the monster other than to gain its attention. The monster began moving towards her. The running charge was replaced by a staggering limp due to the impact with the cave wall.

When the monster had completely turned its back on the group, Mirka made his move. He darted off towards the beast with the odd-looking rope in his hands. As he got close, he began to swing the end of the rope round and round like a cowboy trying to lasso a bull.

The rock monster had closed the distance to Zyanya and appeared to have her cornered. It swung one huge, clawed rock hand towards her but caught nothing more than air as Zyanya vanished reappearing to the right of the monster. At the same time, Mirka let go of the rope, and it wrapped itself around the monster's legs getting tighter on its own. The rock monster roared and looked down at its legs. It clawed at the rope but was unable to move it. Mirka held the other end and pulled tightly trying to bring down the beast.

Arto understood the plan and raced to help him. The others soon joined in. Grabbing the rope, they pulled with all their might and the rock monster lost its balance and collapsed to the ground. The impact rocked the whole cave. Cracks appeared beneath the monster and spread quickly.

'Run!' shouted Granddad.

The others needed no further encouragement and ran as fast as they could past the stunned monster. George fired off a couple of liquid nitrogen bombs for good measure as he ran. Both hit the monster freezing its head and good arm. Still, the monster did not move.

The crack in the cave continued to grow, and suddenly the whole cave system was shaking and moving. Cracks appeared on the cave walls, and the one on the floor widened every second. The rock monster lay across the large crack. It began to come round and started to try and stand. The rope was still tightly wound around its legs, and the crack in the cave floor didn't help. The monster stumbled forward and collapsed again. Part of the cave roof began to crumble as the cracks reached that high. Large sections began to fall as the group continued to run increasing the distance between themselves and the monster.

Arto looked back just as a huge section of cave roof smashed into the rock monster severing the head from the body. More and more rock tumbled on top of the monster. The cave floor gave way, and the monster was lost into the chasm that had been created.

Arto caught up with the others and urged them to run faster.

'The whole cave system is going to collapse. We need to get out of here now!' He roared.

The group didn't look back and ran until their lungs and legs ached. They could hear the terrible noise of stone smashing into stone and could feel the vibrations every time a part of the caves collapsed. George was terrified; he was convinced the noises were getting closer. He turned and glanced briefly behind them without stopping. He could see nothing apart from a huge dust cloud that was catching them quickly. It looked like some kind of monster the way it moved and swallowed everything in its way.

Daylight up ahead let them know they were close to the surface and gave the group the hope they needed that they could get out of the caves. They found extra energy to run faster and harder towards the light. Bursting out of the caves they didn't stop running. Led by Arto they kept going until they could no longer see the opening to this side of the caves. They began to climb as they ran as the ground took them away from the caves towards the city.

Only when they were convinced that they were safe did Arto stop and look behind them. Peter joined the huge bear and watched as the ground above the cave system collapsed, and a huge dust cloud fell over the whole area. It was like watching a report of a terrible earthquake on the news.

The Elders collapsed, breathing hard and fast, unable to stand up any longer.

'One thing's for sure, we'll need to find another way back.' George said as he came to stand next to Peter. He leant on his friend and tried to catch his breath.

Peter looked at George and could see how scared he looked despite his joking comments.

'It's ok, we brought a boat.' Peter replied with a smile.

Chapter 14

The Master and Charlotte heard the commotion coming from above them. The sound of goblins and trolls running and shouting excitedly to one another. They left the room and made their way back towards the pathway to the surface.

'What's going on?' Charlotte asked.

'I've no idea, but they don't usually get this excited unless there's a feast or execution.' The Master replied.

They came through the hidden door behind the cauldron just as a large group of goblins ran past heading for the pathway. They saw the Master and stopped running unsure what to do instead.

'Where's everyone going?' the Master asked the nearest goblin.

'Something is happening on the edge of the city, something huge!' the goblin replied in an excited half-shouting voice.

'Who told you this?'

'It's come from the watch towers.'

'What exactly are they saying?'

'The world is crumbling!'

'That makes no sense.' The Master replied. She turned to Charlotte who clearly didn't make any sense of it either.

'Come on Charlotte, let's see what's happening.'

The Master took Charlotte's hand, and they both vanished. The goblins looked around at each other before screeching and running up the pathway.

The trolls on the lookout towers were sounding horns and pointing frantically to the edge of the city. The lead troll on the west lookout tower was barking orders for runners to go in every direction. He turned to bark another order and found himself staring directly at the Master.

'What's happening?' the Master asked.

'Over there, something has happened. It looks like the ground has collapsed.' The troll answered.

Charlotte and the Master moved over to the side of the tower and looked to where the troll had pointed. A large cloud was beginning to disperse, and they could see a huge, jagged canyon had appeared which had begun to fill with water from the river, diverting its very course.

'The caves have collapsed. Jacob is coming.' The Master said.

'Master, if Jacob and his group were in those caves then surely they will be dead.' The head troll replied.

'No. Something tells me they will be very much alive, and if they are through the caves, they are getting close to us.'

'Master, nothing could survive such a collapse.' The troll responded, giving the Master a doubtful look as if he didn't believe a word she was saying.

The Master looked at the troll then to Charlotte. Her expression changed, and she turned her attention back to the troll. Without a word, she thrust both hands towards the troll who was thrown from the guard tower taking two others with him. The trolls screamed as they plummeted towards the ground.

'Does anyone else think I might be wrong?' the Master asked the remaining trolls.

They all shook their heads and looked everywhere but at the Master.

'Good, now who is second in command at this tower?' she asked.

'I am Master.' Said a small fat troll who edged forward slowly.

'Send runners to the barracks; tell them the Master instructs them to send an army to the south of the city. The enemy that caused that collapse is heading our way and we must defend ourselves.'

*****

Peter stood next to his Granddad as they both looked at the massive canyon that had opened where the caves had been.

'If they had any doubt we were coming, they don't now.' Granddad said looking at Peter.

'We should keep moving. You're right Jacob they will know we are nearby, and they will waste no time in sending someone to find us.' Mirka said from behind them.

Porr and Tofi stood next to Arto and surveyed the road ahead of them. They were in a forest which had several dirt roads cut into it. They could see somewhere up ahead the strange glowing light that flowed into the sky.

'How close are we to the city?' Arto asked Mirka.

'Not far. The middle path could get us there in an hour. That's if nothing is coming the other way.' Mirka replied.

'I think it's certain that something will be coming the other way.' Arto replied growling towards the path.

'They are likely to send an army this time. Something capable of killing us all.' Mirka stated.

'Then we must not get caught.' Granddad said as he walked over to Arto and viewed the path ahead.

Peter looked at the path and the forest that surrounded it. The trees were so burnt and dead they looked like the slightest touch would turn them to dust. They were thick though and close together. Anything could hide in the forest if it did it in the right way. He walked over to the nearest tree and ran his hand across the trunk. He looked at his fingertips and saw they were coated in dark burnt bark which stuck to his skin. Peter smiled and turned to the others.

'I have an idea.' He said showing them his hands.

Peter explained his idea and soon they were all going over to the trees and covering themselves in the dead bark dust. They ran it through their hair and over their clothes. Standing on the path, they looked ridiculous but as soon as they moved into the trees, they were much harder to spot.

The Elders helped each other making sure their camouflage worked. George threw dust and dead tree all over Peter's back who then did the same in return. Arto walked past the tree line and found a small opening where the ground was covered in bark and burnt leaves. He lay down and rolled himself over and over until enough of the bark covered him.

George tapped Peter on the shoulder and pointed at the bear.

'Would you like me to scratch your tummy for you?' he asked as Arto lay on his back.

'Only if you'd like me to eat your arm.' Arto replied showing his teeth to George as he did.

The group looked at each other, and every one of them was fairly well camouflaged apart from Zyanya who had not joined in.

'Are you going to join us?' Peter asked looking at Zyanya.

She didn't answer. She just looked at Peter and vanished then reappeared behind him and tapped him on the shoulder.

'Do you think I need to hide?' she asked before walking away.

The others laughed, even Porr and Tofi let out a little laughter. Peter could feel the skin on his face burning and was glad for the dark tree bark that hid this from the others.

'You're so smooth. I think she'll ask you to be her boyfriend any time now.' George said as he placed his arm around Peter.

'Every time I open my mouth to talk to her, I say something unbelievably stupid.' Peter replied looking down at his feet.

'It wasn't that bad. Asking a girl that can turn invisible if she needs camouflage is an easy mistake to make.'

George said patting Peter on the back and stifling a laugh.

Peter aimed a heel kick at George's ankle. George let out a small cry as Peter's kick made contact. George bent down to rub his ankle when they heard the first sounds of something approaching.

The unmistakable grunts and shrieks of trolls and goblins began to reach them. The group ran to either side of the path and hid in amongst the trees. When everyone was in place, Peter looked around him and found it hard to pick anyone out. He looked over to the other side where the Elders, Mirka and Zyanya were hiding, and the only person he could see was Zyanya. She looked directly at him then vanished for a second and reappeared. She smiled and put one finger to her lips reminding him to be quiet. Peter smiled back.

The trolls and goblins were full of confidence due to their huge numbers. The Master's orders had been very clear; kill everyone apart from the boy and the Viking. The rest should be shown no mercy. They had brought six banshee dogs with them. These were large and powerful dark grey dogs with ice blue eyes, and sensitive noses that they used to sniff out enemies. The dogs were held on leather leashes which attached to metal collars. The banshee dogs growled and barked excitedly as they pulled their troll handlers along the path.

Peter watched Zyanya as her expression changed from one of confidence to one of fear. She strung her bow and glanced towards him before vanishing once again. Then he heard the growling and barking of what he thought were dogs only he had never heard barks as deep or as vicious sounding.

Suddenly he understood the look on Zyanya's face. Dogs could mean they were being tracked, and this would mean no amount of camouflage would keep them safe. They had little choice, though; if they moved now the whole approaching army would see them. They had to stay still and pray the dogs didn't notice them.

The banshee dogs began to howl and pull even harder on their leashes.

'Let them go!' shouted the head troll.

The dogs were set free and began sniffing widely at the path and running back and forth. Peter stood motionless as two of the biggest dogs he had ever seen shot past heading down towards the caves. He had never seen anything like them. He dared not even look at George who he knew was hiding right next to him.

Four dogs had run past, and now they could hear the troll army getting very close. Peter was beginning to believe that the dogs had missed them and were leading the army to the caves when he heard the dead tree bark behind him snap and break. The deep snarl that followed froze Peter to the spot.

The banshee dog approached slowly. The hackles raised up on its neck as the scent of the enemy got stronger. Its sense of smell was amazing, but its eyesight was poor. It could smell the enemy all around it but could only see the shapes of trees. Slowly it approached the area where the smell was strongest. It sniffed the ground and lifted its head.

The large mouth opened revealing large deadly teeth. A drop of drool clung to the front teeth before falling into the burnt earth. A slight movement to the left and it was sure. The enemy was here. The powerful dog turned its head and saw the briefest flash of eyes from the tree next to it.

The dog lowered itself nearer the ground and was about to leap at the hidden enemy when it heard the faint whistle. The banshee turned in time to take the arrow in the centre of its forehead. It didn't have time to yelp or warn its masters.

Peter dared to move his head and looked behind him. Zyanya was standing with her bow still drawn, and another arrow ready to fire. Peter wondered why she had not put down her bow, when a huge dog burst through the trees to the side of them, running straight for Peter and George. Zyanya shot off two arrows before the dog could reach its target. The enormous beast slumped to the ground without another sound.

Zyanya vanished then reappeared right behind Peter.

'They'll come looking for their dogs soon. We need to move.'

'What are they?' Peter asked.

'Banshee dogs. Their eyesight is terrible, but they can smell an enemy from a great distance. It won't take the other dogs long to realise they missed us.'

The huge troll and goblin army was now further down the path, and the group could hear their frustration growing as they couldn't find their prey. Granddad appeared next to Peter and spoke to them all.

'Zyanya's right, we need to move, and we need to move now. Stay off the path everyone and run as fast as you can.'

No one needed any further encouragement and the groups on either side of the path began to move towards the city, and away from the massive army. The howling of Banshee dogs made them run faster. Had the dogs realised they had missed them and were now beginning the chase?

George was thinking this very thought when he tumbled to the ground thinking he had caught his foot on a root. He went to free his foot and found that it was being held by the dark green hand of a goblin who was hiding amongst the dead undergrowth. George struggled and fought, worried about using the shooter from such close range. The goblin had a crude dagger in its free hand and was about to strike down on George when Peter's sword removed its head.

'Come on; we need to keep running!' Peter shouted.

Suddenly the world was full of movement as more goblins and trolls appeared from their hiding places and began to chase the group. Peter and George could see the explosions of sunshine bombs from the other side of the path and hear the screams of pain from the dying creatures.

Arto roared as he took down trolls with huge swipes of his front paws. George looked behind them and saw twenty or so trolls giving chase. He fired off some shots from both arms hoping to take down as many as he could.

Some were frozen while others were dropped by the arrow heads, but still, they came. He watched as Zyanya appeared and killed five trolls before leaping across to the other side to help Mirka and the Elders.

Granddad fought side by side with Porr and Tofi. The attack had come so quickly that he had not had a chance to get back to Peter and George. They had been wrong to think the troll army would be easily outsmarted. His sword was thick with their blood, and his shield was damaged by the sheer amount of dagger and axe strikes it had taken.

Peter and George caught up to where Granddad and his brothers were fighting and joined the battle. It was as if the forest had suddenly been replaced by a sea of trolls and goblins. George fired off shot after shot killing scores of them, but still, they came from every direction.

'Go to the path and run as fast as you can! There's no point in hiding anymore!' Granddad shouted.

Led by Arto, who smashed a hole through the enemy, they fled through the dead trees until they reached the path, killing any enemies they met. As they reached the path, the Elders and Mirka came running out of the other side. Elder Thomson stumbled and fell to the ground heavily. He had a cut on his forehead, and his nose was bleeding. Elder Sanderson had fared no better and was covered in cuts and scrapes.

'Ogres, there are ogres everywhere!' Elder Thomson shouted as he got to his feet.

The group ran as they heard the sound of growls and shrieks all around them. Ogres burst out of one side as trolls and goblins came from the other. Zyanya would appear for a few seconds and kill three or four before vanishing again. The mysterious girl clearly scared the enemy who screamed in terror each time she appeared.

They kept running with the enemy chasing behind them. The Elders threw sunshine bombs over their shoulders killing scores of goblins, ogres and trolls and slowing down the others around them. The combination of the bombs and Zyanya's arrows was enough to keep the enemy at bay as they ran for the city.

Finally, they could see it. A large wall made from the trunks of huge trees ran around the perimeter of the city. The path led to an entrance gate that lay open. The group saw the entrance and ran faster spurred on by the hope it offered.

When they were all through, they ran to the large wheels that operated the gates and began to close them. The Elders, Zyanya and Mirka stood at the gates and fired off sunshine bombs and arrows as quickly as they could. The gates closed and Porr, Tofi, Peter and George put the huge logs across the back of the gate, locking it from the inside.

The enemy smashed off the gate over and over but was unable to break in. The barking of Banshee dogs could be heard mixed in with the screeches and growls.

'We must've killed hundreds of them and still there are so many left.' Elder Thomson said.

'That gate will not hold them forever.' Granddad said watching as the gate shook violently.

'There's something else to think about.' Peter said turning his attention away from the gate.

'Which is?' George asked.

'We've locked them out, but we've also locked us in with whatever lives in this city.' Peter replied.

The group turned and looked at the city. The strange beam of light looked more amazing from this close. The colour and the strange pulses were hypnotic.

'As we thought, it looks like it's coming from the centre of the city.' Mirka said.

'Then that's where we're going.' Replied Arto.

'Mirka, can you get us there and keep us off the main paths?' Granddad asked.

'Yes, I should be able to.'

'Good. We have to assume they know we are here, but with their main army stuck outside maybe we can get there without too much trouble.' Granddad said then motioned to Mirka to lead the way.

Chapter 15

The Master watched from the tower as the army swarmed at the gate. She shook her head in disappointment.

'They are useless. They must outnumber them a hundred to one and yet they find themselves locked out of their city.'

'What should we do now?' Charlotte asked looking from the Master to the distant army.

'I have a plan Charlotte, a plan that involves you. Are you willing to help me get the victory we want?' The Master stared into Charlotte's eyes as she spoke.

'Of course I am, just let me know what I can do.'

'Good, we won't have much time until Jacob and the others arrive. We must be ready for them. Come quickly. I will tell you the plan as we go.'

James sat in his cell. There wasn't anything else he could do. He had heard the commotion and thought he had felt the ground shake at one point. No one had come to take him away or rescue him. There was no news on Charlotte, and that was what made him lose the most hope. His sister was beyond his help.

He heard the familiar gruff voices of trolls coming closer.

'She's heavier than she looks.'

'Just take her back to the cell like the Master asked.'

'Why does she want her back in there?'

'Maybe she's of no use now. Or maybe we are going to get to eat them both!'

The trolls continued to discuss various ways of cooking children before one of them opened the cell door and Charlotte was thrown inside. She landed heavily on the floor and didn't move.

'Charlotte!' cried James as he ran over to his sister. He gently lifted her head and rested it against his chest as he cradled her.

'What have they done to you? Wake up, please wake up.'

Charlotte slowly opened her eyes. She seemed confused and groggy but began to come round. She looked around her with startled eyes until she saw James.

'What happened to you? I thought I'd never see you again.' James said.

'The Master, she tried to get me to join her. She wanted me to become like her. I refused, and she punished me.' Charlotte said.

'Why did she let you go?'

'Peter and his Granddad are in the city. They've shut the army outside, and the Master got worried. She ordered the trolls to put me back in here with you until she has defeated them.'

'They're here? They've got this close?' James asked.

'Yes, somehow they collapsed a cave system and evaded the army and are coming for us.' Charlotte smiled as she spoke.

'What did the Master do to you?'

'She threw me into the light. The pain was so great, but I refused to join her.' Charlotte replied.

'They'll save us Charlotte, and we can go home.'

'Oh, I hope so James. I really do.' Charlotte turned away as she spoke and just for a second her eyes flashed yellow.

*****

They moved slowly through small, deserted streets of damaged houses. If Mirka felt any sadness for the destruction all around him, he didn't show it. He was focussed on getting to the centre of the city.

Peter looked around him at the scale of the city and couldn't help but be impressed. It must have taken years to build such a place in the forest. The Master had taken it from them in an instant and destroyed everything they had worked so hard to create. He wondered if that was what she was going to do to his world eventually. Was this her plan, to move from world-to-world conquering and destroying?

Mirka, Zyanya and Granddad walked at the front of the group with Arto at the back. The large bear had not been happy about this, but Mirka had explained that it would be easier to move unseen if Mirka could make sure the path was clear before a huge warrior bear was spotted walking towards the centre of the city. Arto had reluctantly agreed.

Mirka raised his hand, and they all stopped. The group stood silently as Mirka and Zyanya moved forward alone. Without warning Zyanya vanished and reappeared on the top of one of the burnt-out houses. She looked around, then at Mirka and signalled three with her left her hand. Zyanya took two arrows out and strung them both.

Mirka turned to the others and signalled for them to stay where they were. He walked out to the middle of the road where it joined another at a crossroads. Instantly the growls of goblins could be heard. The goblins closed in on Mirka who drew his sword leaving his bow behind his back.

'There's three of us against one of you,' one of the goblins sneered as they approached with their short, crooked swords drawn.

Before Mirka could reply, he heard the sound of Zyanya's bow being released and watched as two of the goblins fell lifeless to the ground.

'Now it's just you and me,' Mirka said to the goblin who was no longer so confident.

The goblin looked around for the hidden archer who had killed its companions. It looked at Mirka and his sword. The goblin looked at his sword, screamed and ran away in the direction he had come. The goblin had run about fifty yards when the arrow landed squarely in its back. Zyanya appeared and retrieved her arrows from the fallen goblins.

Mirka signalled the others to come. George and Peter walked past the fallen bodies of the goblins.

'She makes it look so easy.' Peter said staring at Zyanya.

'She can make herself invisible. That must help.' George replied.

'I wonder how she does that.' Peter asked.

'No idea, but I wish I could.' George answered.

Mirka waited for the others to gather round.

'The goblins were coming down this path and judging by a number of footprints on it I would say it is the one they use the most. If we take this other path to the side we can get to the centre very quickly, but then we will have those watch towers to deal with,' he said and pointed over towards the beam of light.

'Zyanya can help us with that, but you all have to play your part.' He continued.

They all agreed without having any idea how they could help. Slowly and quietly, they made their way closer and closer to the watch towers. The day was giving way to night, and the semi-darkness was helping hide their progress from the enemy.

They could see the watch towers and Arto's eyesight allowed him to pick out five trolls on the ground near the towers. Mirka and Zyanya killed all five quickly and quietly with their arrows.

'Peter and Jacob stand at the base of that tower.' Mirka said pointing over to the furthest watch tower.

'Porr and Tofi, you go to the one over there. George, Elders and Arto we can't use you for this.'

'Why not?' growled Arto.

'George your weapons are no use at such close quarters, and neither are yours, Elders. Arto you'll see why we can't use you.'

Mirka said no more and moved to position himself beside one of the towers. With everyone in place, Zyanya approached Peter and his Granddad.

'Draw your swords and take my hand. You must be ready as soon as I let go of your hands, you will have to fight.'

'What do you mean?' Peter asked looking confused.

'Take my hand Peter and trust me.' Zyanya replied and smiled.

They both took her hands, and she looked at them and nodded. The world went black for a second and Peter had the sensation of rushing through the air. Suddenly the world reappeared, and he and Granddad were on the watch tower along with four startled looking trolls.

Granddad snapped out of it quickest and moved to kill the nearest trolls. Peter shook his head and joined in. The trolls were so surprised that they barely had time to draw their weapons before they were all dead. They watched the commotion happening on the other towers as one by one they were all cleared of enemies. Zyanya cleared the last one on her own within seconds.

'How do we get down?' Peter asked his Granddad.

'The same way you got up.' Replied Zyanya appearing behind them.

With everyone back on the ground, Zyanya turned to Arto.

'I'm sorry Arto, but I couldn't lift you like I can lift the others.' She said.

The large bear growled and turned away.

'Is he sulking?' George asked the Elders.

The Elders shrugged and watched Arto stride away.

Peter was standing next to his Granddad watching the beam of light. The strange red glow with the purple pulses was hypnotic. They stared down into the huge hole in the ground and could see the light was coming from far beneath them.

Mirka joined them and watched the light. He looked at the spiral walkway that ran around it.

'This is where they attacked. The ground just vanished. There was no warning no sign that they were coming. They've been busy.' Mirka said.

'If James and Charlotte are here then they are down there somewhere. We need to get to them.' Granddad said.

They heard the first noises from beneath them and watched as the bottom of the walkway began to swarm with activity. They heard the screeches of goblins and the growling of trolls.

'Now it's my turn!' Roared Arto.

The large bear charged down the walkway towards the approaching enemy. The others gave chase and followed Arto.

The trolls at the front could see the large bear charging towards them and had nowhere to run. The trolls and goblins behind were driving them on, not allowing them to turn around.

Arto smashed into the trolls and sent them flying over both sides of the walkway. His roars were deafening as he continued through the trolls and goblins. Any that managed to escape the bear had to face the group charging down behind him. Peter fought side by side with his Granddad killing the odd enemy that Arto missed.

Arto killed scores of enemies; most died falling from the walkway while others were trampled underfoot. He took several hits but felt nothing as the thrill of the battle took hold. Warrior bears were born for moments like this.

They reached the bottom very quickly. The trolls and goblins that were left began to run back into the darkness of the caves; terrified by Arto, they had no desire for this fight.

Peter looked at the huge cauldron that was the source of the light. It looked simple, yet the beam of light was so mysterious and powerful he thought there must be some dark magic at work here. Something told him not to touch the light.

The group took in their surroundings. The cave system went in both directions away from the cauldron. The trolls and goblins had all fled to the left-hand side which made them think James and Charlotte would be that way as well.

They went forward cautiously with Arto at the front as his eyes were quickest at adjusting to the change in light. The eerie silence was more unnerving than the sound of the trolls and goblins running up the walkway towards them. They huddled closer together as they walked. No one spoke, and everyone was on their guard.

The group had no idea they were being watched. The Master was close by watching them move through the dark. Her eyes fell on the girl. It couldn't be her, after all, these years she had come back. Did she know who she was? The Master wasn't the only one watching.

When the attack came, it came so quickly that none of them were ready. The large grey monster seemed to emerge from out of the wall and smashed Arto across the cave floor with one powerful strike. It roared then attacked the others.

Porr and Tofi met the attack head on, using their shields to deflect the blows while trying to inflict damage with their swords. This enemy was too strong and too quick. Porr was batted away like a fly, and Tofi's sword was caught in one powerful hand, and the metal was crushed in front of their eyes. Tofi tried to hit the beast with his shield, but this had no effect, and the creature picked him up and crushed the life out of him in seconds.

Granddad yelled with rage and attacked. He matched the monster for speed and was able to evade the savage blows and inflict some of his own. The sword strikes annoyed the monster rather than hurt it. Peter ran in to help, while Mirka and Zyanya fired arrow after arrow at the beast.

George waited for his moment then when a chance presented itself, he fired off several of the arrowheads into the monster. It was thrown back and landed heavily on the ground. Elder Thomson threw a sunshine bomb for good measure which exploded on the beast.

'It's the Shifter!' Elder Sanderson said. 'This is the form it was in when it attacked the ship,' he continued.

Elder Thomson ran over to Arto who was coming to his senses and getting back to his feet. Tofi was dead, and Porr seriously hurt. Mirka approached the unmoving monster and kicked it with his foot. There was no reaction.

'I think you killed him, George. Those arrowheads are proving…'

Mirka didn't get to finish his sentence as the beast rose up behind him and with one mighty blow smashed him against the cave wall. Mirka fell lifeless to the ground. It looked at them all, finally resting its eyes on George.

'When will you realise the truth. You cannot kill me. Nothing you do hurts me. Everything you do makes me stronger!' The Shifter roared.

Zyanya looked at Mirka lying still on the floor and attacked the beast. Arrow after arrow hit home. The beast roared and charged at her. Zyanya vanished just in time then fired off more arrows from her new position. The beast charged again and again. Each time Zyanya vanished then attacked just out of reach of the Shifter.

The Shifter would let her win one more time then he would let her in on his secret. The girl evaded his clutches and fired off another couple of arrows. The pain was annoying, nothing more. He went for her again and this time when she vanished, he grabbed her out of the air. The look on her face was priceless. The Shifter smiled the coldest smile Zyanya had ever seen.

'Can I tell you a secret? When you disappear, I can still see you.' The Shifter opened his mouth to show the girl his razor-sharp teeth.

'You don't seem so confident now little girl. It's time to say goodbye to your friends. Don't worry they'll be joining you soon.'

The Shifter lifted Zyanya above his head and was about to smash her off the ground when his expression changed. Peter wasn't sure if it was surprise or pain, but the monster dropped Zyanya and turned around.

They couldn't see who the Shifter was looking at or what had happened. There didn't seem to be any wounds, but he was clearly in a lot of pain. The Shifter roared and screamed, falling to his knees. Whatever was doing this was causing more damage than any of them were able to. Blood came from the nose, eyes, mouth and ears.

Finally, the Shifter stopped screaming and lay still. The skin began to harden and turn at first to rock and then began to crumble to dust. The Shifter had been killed by something, but none of them knew what.

The Master had watched in horror as the Shifter had plucked Zyanya from out of thin air. She had no choice; she had to protect her. She had to decide which life was more valuable. It was an easy choice. The Shifter was a great warrior, but unreliable, and Zyanya was her daughter. She used her magic to kill the Shifter. He was wrong; there was one person alive who could kill him; there would be no coming back from this.

The group were stunned. No one dared to move. Something had just killed the Shifter right in front of them. It didn't appear to be a trick. The dust that was once the Shifter swirled around the cave floor.

'What happened?' George asked.

'I've no idea. Something killed him.' Elder Sanderson replied feeling a bit silly for stating the obvious.

'I'm glad because we weren't doing so well on that front.' George replied.

'I'm not sure glad is what we should be.' Peter said.

'Why not? He's dead.' Replied George.

'There's something in these caves that can kill the Shifter without showing itself. That terrifies me.' Peter said watching all around them as he did.

Granddad knelt by the body of Tofi and said a soft, silent prayer. Another of his brothers was lost to him. Porr was getting to his feet and being given medicine by the Elders. Arto seemed dazed but otherwise ok. Zyanya was by the body of Mirka. She touched his face as tears ran down hers.

'We'll take him back with us.' Peter said from behind her.

'We can't carry any bodies back. It's dangerous enough without more of us unable to fight.' She replied.

'Zyanya, Peter's right. We will take him back to your people. Arto can carry him.'

Arto nodded his huge head in response.

'We must move on, though, we can't afford to spend a minute longer here than we need to.' Granddad said. 'It's time to find James and Charlotte and get out of here.' He continued.

'What about the cauldron? Shouldn't we try and stop it?' Peter asked.

Zyanya needed no encouragement and fired off three arrows at the cauldron. None hit their target they all seemed to be deflected away. George stood forward and sent a blast from both hands towards it. Neither blast had any effect as they appeared to die just before they reached the cauldron.

'There must be something protecting it. We have to move on; we're not going to be able to do anything about the cauldron from here.' Granddad said.

Reluctantly the others agreed, and they began to walk through the dark, damp cave system looking for any sign of their friends. The whole place seemed deserted. There were no trolls or goblins. No ogres or barclues, there was nothing here. The quiet was so eerie, so complete that they could hear the echo of their footsteps and the constant dripping of water running down the cave walls. A place that had been alive with enemies was now still.

Then they saw it, the single wooden door in the cave wall. Bolted from the outside, but with no guards anywhere near it.

'James, Charlotte, are you in there?' whispered Peter at the door.

'Peter is that you?' The response was quiet and unsure, but it was James's voice.

'James, we've found you. Is Charlotte there too?'

'Yes, I'm here. I can't believe you found us. Get us out of here Peter please.' Her voice had a scared pleading sound to it.

Granddad opened the door, and the children rushed out to their saviours. They hugged their friends and were checked by the Elders who were glad to see they both seemed fine. Charlotte told them about the Master taking her away and trying to get her to join the enemy.

'If you hadn't arrived in the city when you did, who knows what would have happened.' She said with tears streaming down her face.

'Thankfully you don't have to worry about that because we are here now, and we're taking you both out of here.' Granddad replied.

Granddad looked at James and then back to Charlotte before continuing.

'Charlotte, when the Master took you away, did she tell you anything about this place. Is there another way out? I don't want to go back through the city. The troll army will be through the gates by now.'

'I can't remember, I don't think so.' Charlotte said. She looked confused, and as if she was trying hard to remember any small detail.

'Wait, there was something. There's an entrance further down this tunnel. It takes you near a bridge. I can't remember its name.' Charlotte looked to the others for help.

'Travellers' Pass. It must be Travellers' Pass.' Said Zyanya. The others agreed.

'You've done well Charlotte; you could have saved us another fight.' Granddad said smiling at Charlotte.

'Let's move. I don't like this quiet, it doesn't feel right, but while it's here we should make the best of it,' he said to all of them. They started to move off quickly in search of the way out to Travellers' Pass.

Good girl, good girl. The Master watched from the darkness. Charlotte was playing the role excellently. Take them over the pass and back to their forest. Then her plan could move to the final stage. She looked at Zyanya walking next to the bear. She looked so small compared to the huge beast. The Master would ensure no harm would come to Zyanya. Anyone that tried to hurt her would suffer the same fate as the Shifter.

Chapter 16

They came out of the caves into the dead of night. Darkness surrounded them, and the light from the stars was dulled by the redness created by the cauldron. They dared not use any torches as they didn't want to draw attention to themselves.

They could hear the river, so they knew they were not far from the bridge. Arto took the lead once more. His keen eyesight cut through the darkness that surrounded the others. As they approached the bridge, they heard voices coming from nearby. They stopped walking and kept listening. Five trolls came marching from their left.

'What makes anyone think they would come this way? No one but us has used Travellers' Pass in years.' One of them said in a low grunting tone.

'I think we should be happy; it keeps us out the way of that bear. Have you seen the size of his teeth?' a large fat troll replied.

Arto looked at George and showed him his teeth and seemed to smile. Zyanya whispered something to the bear then moved ahead.

The five trolls would lead them right to the bridge as long as they stayed back and remained quiet.

'Let's just get to the bridge and stand guard like they asked. I'd rather be here than at the docks with the rest of them waiting on that fancy ship of theirs and having to face the Viking.' A smaller troll joined the conversation.

'Oh, and don't forget those teeth. This is a much safer job.' The fat one added.

Before long the trolls arrived at the bridge and after some arguing and a couple of knocks on the head it was decided that the three smaller ones would cross and guard the other side while the two larger ones remained at this side.

'This suits me. I can't be bothered walking across the bridge. What's the point? No one is going to come this way.' The largest and fattest troll said as he watched the others walk away.

When there was no response to his wise words, he looked at his companion and gave him a shove.

'Not asleep already are you?' he asked.

The troll wasn't asleep. When he was shoved, he simply fell forward, and the other troll saw the arrow in his neck. Before he could scream or alert the others, he felt a dull thud in his chest and looked down to see the arrow buried in him. The last thing he would ever see as his life slipped away was a ghostly girl appear from nowhere then vanish just as quickly.

The three smaller trolls were still bickering about whose fault it was that they got sent to the other side. They didn't notice the girl advancing towards them. Even if they had, they would have been able to do nothing about it. Zyanya strung three arrows in one movement and released them without breaking stride. All three trolls dropped to the ground. Zyanya retrieved her arrows as the others joined her.

'I can lead us from here. We're not far from my home now.' She said to the others before turning around and starting to walk down the path.

After about twenty minutes they arrived at the mouth of the cave system they had entered earlier. It seemed like days ago to Peter. This side of the cave had fared better than the part that had collapsed. It looked the same as it had before only the roof was lower.

James and Charlotte walked next to Granddad and Porr the whole way. They wouldn't leave their side. George walked with them as well. He had made a vow to himself to protect Charlotte and get her home. He couldn't believe she had almost been turned by the Master. If anything tried to harm her, he would use his shooter until there was nothing left to defend her with.

The familiar surroundings made the group move faster and soon they were moving through the forest and heading towards the safety of the tribespeople. Elder Sanderson felt confident and relieved. They were almost back and had saved the children. He looked around and found a large branch lying on the ground. He took out some liquid sunshine and dropped a small amount onto the branch. Within seconds they were lit up.

'Get rid of it!' shouted Granddad.

Elder Sanderson looked confused.

'There's no one else here Jacob, we are going to be fine.' He replied.

The deafening and chilling roar of the barclue was far too close for comfort. The group didn't need to hear a second roar to start running. They could hear the trees being smashed behind them as the barclue searched for its prey.

It roared again and this time, the roar was answered by two other distinct roars from either side of them. They were being hunted and surrounded by the huge beasts. Charlotte began to cry as she was dragged along by Porr. James kept running, trying desperately to keep up with the others.

They reached the clearing that was still full of the bodies of their enemies from the earlier battle. The roar from in front of them stopped them in their tracks. They were surrounded on all sides.

The barclue behind them came into the clearing as did the ones to their left and right. The large beasts roared and beat the ground edging closer all the time. George stood beside Charlotte as the one at their back got closer. It seemed to be looking at her and ignoring the others. It moved its head from side to side and sniffed the air. It hesitated; all of a sudden this large beast seemed unsure of itself.

The other barclues appeared to sense the hesitation and stopped moving forward. They began to roar at each other as if they were talking. The group had nowhere to run, and all they could do was watch these huge vicious beasts as they became increasingly animated. Peter had no idea what to make of it as he stood with his sword drawn ready to fight.

Zyanya stood motionless next to Arto with her bow strung ready to attack the first barclue that made a move. The move the barclues made took them all by surprise. One by one the barclues turned and walked away back into the forest.

No one moved; no one knew what to do.

'What just happened?' Peter asked.

'I've no idea. What would make barclues act like that?' Granddad asked the question to himself, but all eyes turned to Zyanya.

'I've never seen anything like that before. I've never seen them hesitate never mind retreat.'

George said nothing; he didn't tell the others he had seen the way the barclue had looked at Charlotte before it turned away. He tried to tell himself it was the sight of the shooter that had killed the other barclues that had scared them off. He tried to tell himself this, but he knew it wasn't true.

'Whatever the reason we need to move, we are very close to safety.' Granddad said before moving forward.

Peter ran to catch up with him and put his hand on his Granddad's arm.

'There's a lot of very strange things happening. Where did all the trolls go? They ran away somewhere, but we didn't see any in the caves. Why was the pass so badly guarded? Where's the Master? Where's Tolldruck? Does this not seem a little too easy?' He whispered his questions.

'I've been thinking the same thing, asking myself the same questions. This isn't the first time the Master has had me guessing what her plans are.'

'How are we going to get home? We didn't find out how to work the portals; we have no prisoners to take us across.'

'We need to get your friends safe then we can work that out.'

'I don't like this Granddad; something's very wrong here.'

'Keep on your guard Peter, I don't disagree with you, but our priority was to make sure James and Charlotte were safe. Once we have completed that task, we can start to think about the others that lie ahead of us.'

Peter tried to smile at his Granddad, but there was no conviction in it. Something wasn't right and whatever it was scared him.

The group moved forward unchallenged by any enemy. The brief encounter with the barlcues and the five trolls on the pass were the only things they had faced. They could see the protected area now and walked faster because of it. From inside the area, archers appeared. They watched the group approach and were ready to protect them from any enemy. No enemy came, and the group arrived safely.

Melissa came forward to meet them holding Jake in her arms. Jake squirmed and wriggled when he saw Peter and tried every move he knew to get to him. He wiggled this way and that way and finally Jake resorted to licking wildly at her face. This made Melissa let go, and Jake ran to Peter who picked up his dog and rubbed his head while avoiding the face licking.

Melissa hugged Granddad as the tribespeople came forward and spoke to Zyanya. They lifted Mirka's body off of Arto and carried him through the forest to the village.

'We've only partly succeeded. We saved the children but there was no sign of the Master, and we are no closer to understanding anything about the portals.' Granddad said to Melissa.

'The children were the most important thing, Jacob. Bringing them to safety was the priority.' She replied.

'We still need to work out how to get home,' he said looking at Charlotte as he did. The girl was looking at her with a peaceful, thoughtful expression. She didn't look scared or worried.

'What is it, Jacob?'

'It's probably nothing; it's just that once we had found the children, there was nothing to stop us bringing them home.'

'You should maybe be thankful for that as it appears your numbers are far less than when you left us.'

'That's true; maybe I am looking too much into it. The children are safe, as are we.'

*****

The four barclues lay dead at her feet. The Master was furious; these beasts had acted only on the instinct she had given them. They had tracked their enemy and were about to kill them when they sensed the evil in Charlotte. Not wanting to displease their Master they had retreated so as not to harm the girl. This had not pleased the Master. Jacob wasn't stupid; he would realise something was very wrong with their actions and would be watching everything much more closely. This could present her with problems. She had killed the barclues without another thought. Her anger had taken hold, and she felt no remorse.

'What happens now Master?' Tolldruck asked.

'We wait for Charlotte to do what we have asked, and when she does we unleash all our power onto the tribespeople. Let's see how strong Jacob is when he loses his wife for the second time.'

'The army is ready and waiting Master although I still can't find the Shifter.'

'You won't find him Tolldruck. You can look for the rest of your life, and you will never find him.'

'What do you mean?'

'I killed him. He was becoming too unreliable, and his actions displeased me. We are better off without him.' The Master said no more on the subject.

Tolldruck looked at the Master and wondered why she would kill the Shifter. Suddenly the answer came to him. The girl, it must have been the girl. Had the Shifter attacked her or threatened her in front of the Master? Tolldruck knew better than to ask any further questions and left the Master to finish preparing the army. The victory they had all been wanting would come soon, and they could finally conquer this world and kill the Viking.

Chapter 17

The children sat at the tables in the middle of the village. James and Charlotte had been checked over, and it appeared they were physically fine, although shaken by their experience. Granddad tried to explain everything to them, and he had taken his time to go over every detail until it made as much sense as possible.

After all, they had been through, and had seen, James and Charlotte seemed to accept Granddad's explanations. They had lots of questions, and each one was answered truthfully.

The mood in the village was sombre with the news of the deaths of the three tribespeople and Tofi. Jeron and Baden had come to speak with them and were interested in the death of the Shifter.

'He turned to dust?' Baden asked.

'Yes, right in front of us. He seemed unstoppable. I thought we were all going to die then suddenly he was in pain and unable to move. He dropped Zyanya and died. We never saw what did it.' Elder Sanderson replied.

'The Master did it.' Jeron said.

'We can't know that for sure.' Baden added quickly giving Jeron a disapproving glance.

'What makes you think it was the Master?' Elder Thomson asked.

'Oh, nothing. It's just, what else could kill such a monster?' Jeron replied.

An odd silence came over them, and Jeron and Baden made their excuses and left the others to return to their underground home.

Charlotte watched the Elders go and then moved over to talk to George.

'They left in a hurry. Where are they going?' she asked.

'That's where they live. It's pretty cool actually. There is a whole system of rooms down there.' George said, pleased he could impress Charlotte with his knowledge.

'Is there? Down there behind that small door?'

'Yes, it's impressive, do you want to see it?'

'Do you think they'd mind if you took me down?'

'I don't think so. They are a little strange and protective of their things, but they should be ok with it.'

George and Charlotte started walking towards the Elders' home. Charlotte kept looking around and was sure no one was paying them any attention which is exactly what she wanted.

They entered the small doorway with George leading the way. Charlotte turned around and closed the door behind them. She smiled to herself, and her eyes flashed yellow for a second. The end to this tribe and the wretched Viking was coming, and she would help bring it.

Epilogue

The Master moved deep underground. Deep below the cauldron, the gemstone and the Mystics. Down and down she went into the shadowy blackness. There was no light but still she moved with confidence and sureness.

She was convinced Charlotte would do her part which meant it was time to wake her greatest creation. She arrived at the deepest part of the cave system. She stood in front of them and began to chant. One by one they woke up. Black soulless eyes stared out from faces that were as black as the darkest night. Mouths opened to reveal black tongues flicking over dark grey teeth. The beasts were huge, bigger than Ogres and possessing powers that only the Master could better.

The Master looked at her new soldiers and smiled.

'Your time has come my children. Soon the battle will be upon us, and nothing will be able to stand in our way.'

The Demons of Darkness had risen, and death to the enemies of the Master was their only intention.

Author's Notes

The journey I have been on since March 2013 has been amazing. Deciding (with encouragement from my wife) to write and release The Viking's Apprentice was one of the proudest moments of personal achievement I have ever experienced. To then release book two, The Master's Revenge, and now book three, Journey to the Other Side has been fantastic. It's been hard work and fun in equal measures. There has been lots of research, late nights and hours spent in front of my netbook. To have achieved number 1 in their genre on Amazon Kindle for both books in the US and UK has surpassed anything I hoped for and makes all the hard work worthwhile.

I enjoy visiting schools and getting the chance to talk to children about my books. Children always tell you exactly what they think which is refreshing. Some of their drawings of characters in my books have been excellent, and some of their ideas for new enemies and plot twists have been very good. I want to thank every school that has invited me along, and my contact details are included at the end if you want to get in touch.

As always I have a list of people to thank. Writing a book is not a one-man job (well not in my experience).

I would like to thank my editor, Karen, for all her hard work, suggestions and brilliant editing which has helped improve my books, and my punctuation!

I would like to say a big thank you to Joey Franks for her time, advice and patience in answering my constant questions.

Thank you to my amazing artist Ash. Ash designed the covers for The Master's Revenge and Journey to the Other Side and I'm delighted to say is on board for the rest of the series. His contact details are at the end of the book. His cover for The Master's Revenge won 'Children's Book Cover of the Year 2013' in the authorsdb.com competition.

Thank you to each and every one of you that has purchased this book, or the previous two. I love hearing from you through my blog, email, Facebook and twitter. Your constant support and messages telling me how much you enjoy the books mean the world to me, and I appreciate it so much.

Finally, thank you to Kathleen, who has never doubted and has been in my corner from day one. Without Kathleen The Viking's Apprentice would probably still be a half-finished idea on an old PC in my loft.

Read the prologue to book 4 on the next page.

The Viking's Apprentice IV: The Sword of Vercelli

Prologue

The council of dragons met rarely these days. There had not been the need since they banished the witch's army, and the Shifter. Their world had been peaceful, and the dragons had gone on living as they had done for centuries before.

The portal to the witch world was still open. Unknown to the witches and their hordes, the dragons had their own arrangements with the Mystics. In return for leaving the portal open, and passing on the odd piece of information, the Mystics were allowed to learn the secrets of the great mountain where the ice dragons lived. It was a deal that suited everyone.

As a result of this arrangement the dragons knew all about the Viking arriving, and the chaos that had ensued. The Mystics had become unsettled by the latest development, and it was this development that brought the Dragon Council together. Blane, the ice dragon king, sat on his pile of diamonds looking out at the others who had gathered before him.

'We have not met for many years, but today changes all of that.' He said.

'What has changed?' Delstro, the king of the forest dragons, asked.

'The Mystics have informed me that the Master has awoken the Demons of Darkness.' The ice king replied.

The others took a minute to let this information sink in. Borden, the king of the mountain dragons, spoke next.

'What business is this of ours? There's no need for us to join this fight. Our world is peaceful.'

'How long do you think it will remain peaceful? How long until the Demons are looking to our world?' Blane asked.

'You don't know, you can't even say for sure that the Viking won't defeat them. He's done remarkable things in the past.' Borden replied.

'The Viking can't defeat the Demons of Darkness. We all know that.' Blane looked at Borden, who couldn't meet his gaze.

'There's one way he can defeat them.' Lori, king of the cave dragons, joined the conversation. He looked to Blane then continued.

'I owe my life to the Viking. Without him I would have died in that cave. They deserve our help.'

'We can't rush into another world to join a fight that has nothing to do with us.' Borden replied, refusing to move from his stance.

Lori stepped down from his pile of gold and looked at each dragon king in turn.

'If they need our help, I, for one, will stand side by side with them against our common enemy. Have you forgotten what the Master did to our kind? Have you forgotten the years of misery and needless deaths? The years of slavery? Borden, have you forgotten what lies buried in the treasure cave of my kind?' Lori locked eyes with Borden.

'My race will not join this fight. If you want to lead your brothers and sisters into a battle that has nothing to do with us, go ahead. I vote we close the portal and leave them to their own destiny.' Borden replied, then turned to walk out of the meeting chamber.

Blane watched Borden go, then turned to Lori.

'We will stand with you, and with the Viking, but remember the law of the dragons Lori. We must be asked to join this fight, or the fight must come to us.'

Lori headed back to his cave. He remembered that day the Viking saved his life. He remembered his fight with Tolldruck, a fight he still had the scars from. Lori was determined to help the Viking. The Demons of Darkness were the most formidable enemy the Viking would ever face. Without the help of the dragons the Viking would lose.

Read part 4 today.

The Viking's Apprentice IV: The Sword of Vercelli

Contact Details

You can contact me in any of the following ways.

My website: www.kevinmcleodauthor.com

My email: kevinmcleodauthor@gmail.com

Facebook: www.facebook.com/thevikingsapprentice

Twitter: @bannon1975

You can contact the artist through his email.

Ash-Xd@live.com